To Nicolas,
Happy Reading!
xoxo Mom & Dad

THE LOSER LIST

Written and Illustrated by

H.N. KOWITT

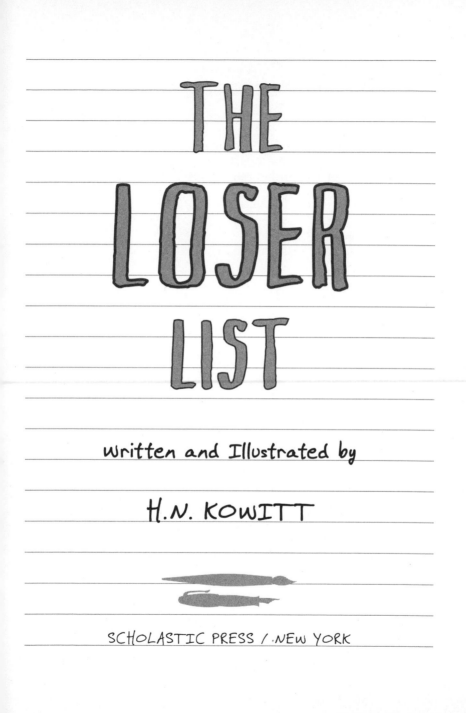

SCHOLASTIC PRESS / NEW YORK

ISBN 978-0-545-24004-8

12 11 10 9 8 7 6 5 4 3 2   11 12 13 14 15 16/0

Printed in the U.S.A.   23

First printing, April 2011

For Mom and Dad

Special thanks to

David Manis and Ellen Miles

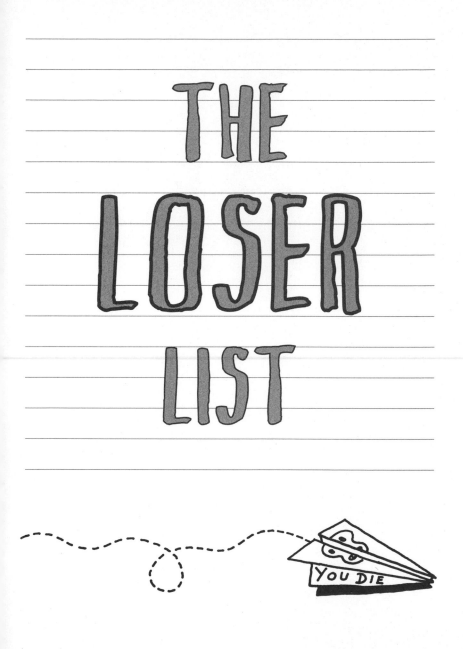

* ME AT-A-GLANCE

Name: Danny Shine (rhymes with "whine")

Age: 12

Occupation: 7th grader at Gerald Ford
   Middle School

Likes to: Draw stuff

Such as: Rusty cans, smelly socks

Hangout: Comix Nation

Impossible crush: Asia O'Neill

Still looking for: A sport I'm good at

Biggest fear: Chantal Davis

Least likely to say: "My fists. Your face."

* CHAPTER ONE *

To be a great artist, you need a great pen. Mine was a T-360, bought for 12 dollars at Abbie's Art Supply.

Who knew it would almost ruin my life?

We were in homeroom, doing a free write. For me, this was a chance to fill my sketchbook with robots and bloody axes. Every few minutes I'd sit back, hoping someone would notice my drawing. "Great X-ray monster," they'd say.

Instead, Chantal Davis poked me.

"Let me see that pen," she said. (Translation: "That pen is mine now.")

"No," I said, putting extra hairs on an eyeball.

Chantal is either a diva, busybody, or bully, depending on how you look at it. You have to watch out, because she can smell fear, and it only makes her madder. If I wasn't so scared of Chantal, I might have a crush on her.

Not the kind of crush I have on, say, Asia O'Neill, the girl in pre-alg with the amazing hair. Chantal is more like a force of nature.

* CHANTAL AT-A-GLANCE

Job: Boss of seventh grade
   (self-appointed)

Plenty of: Attitude

Pet peeve: Doing her own
   homework

Claim to fame: A library
   book that's 6.3 years
   overdue

Quote: "Don't make me
   WHOMP your sorry
   butt."

Chantal's locker is crammed with stuff people have "donated." Well, I'd already given plenty to the Chantal Davis Fund, and I didn't feel like making another contribution. No way was I handing over my T-360.

   Our conversation continued:

Chantal: "NO?"

Me: "No."

Chantal: "Danny, did you not hear what I said?'"

Me: "I heard."

Chantal: "Give me that pen. Or I'll put your name on the Loser List. And then everyone in school will know what a sorry geek you are."

Loser List? Never heard of it.

Chantal went on, "You just drew your last eyeball. When girls see you on the List, they'll cut you dead. You and that crazy troll you hang around." That would be Jasper, my best friend. "Not that anyone talked to you before."

"So?" I gulped. "I'll just cross my name off."

"Yeah?" Chantal whooped. "Next time you're in the GIRLS' BATHROOM?"

Girls' bathroom?

Oh, crud.

Other people looked up, hoping for a fight.

Chantal turned to a guy next to us. "What are you looking at?"

I pretended to laugh off Chantal's threat, but the truth was, it sank in my stomach like a stone. At Gerald Ford, I'm about halfway down the food chain. Not president of the Mathletes, but no one's saving me a seat at the Cool Table. I can't afford a lot of slippage.

* FIVE LISTS MY NAME IS NOT ON:

1. Teen People's Hottest Guys
2. All-City Basketball Team
3. State Science Fair Semifinalists
4. Explorer Scouts' Canoe Portage Sign-up
5. Asia O'Neill's Speed Dial

When the bell rang, I tore out of class to warn Jasper about Chantal. I found him cramming stuff into his locker — math books, a <u>Godzilla</u> DVD, and a small animal carrier.

"Chantal's putting our names on some Loser List," I told him, panting from my sprint. "Telling people we're geeks."

"So?" He shrugged. To him, "geek" isn't an insult. He does his own thing, whether it's magic camp, karaoke chess (don't ask), or inventing weird snow-cone flavors. Jasper is a cool guy, but not everyone can see past his DECIMALS HAVE A POINT T-shirt.

"What's that?" I pointed to the animal carrier.

"Alec's dinner." Jasper has some exotic pets, including a python named Alec Baldwin.

I looked closer. It was a live mouse.

"Miley Cyrus," Jasper said. "Where is this so-called Loser List?"

"Girls' bathroom."

"This is suboptimal?" Jasper stuffed a gerbil wheel on the top shelf.

"What do you — of course!" I sputtered. "You want your geekdom announced to every girl in school?"

Jasper paused. "It's not, like, a secret condition I'm trying to hide."

Well, I'm no geek. I have a wide range of interests:

Reading comics   Drawing comics   Trading comics   Buying comics

In comics, you find a world that's wild and weird, but where the rules are very clear — unlike middle school. Superman <u>knows</u> he can't mess with Kryptonite. My school is weird too, but there's no rule book. You just have to stumble through, hoping you're not committing some crime you were unaware of — wearing the wrong sneakers, say, or liking bluegrass music.

* A FEW THINGS THAT CAN MAKE YOU COOL AT GF:

Sports injury

Your own band

The "right" basketball shoes

video game designer   X-treme Sports champ   Jillionaire

Parent with impossibly cool job

Giant-screen TV

Frontal lobotomy

As the day wore on, I started to think Jasper had the right attitude. We didn't know anything about the list. People might not read it. It could be hard to find, or sloppily written. When I checked out the graffiti in the boys' bathroom, I was reassured by its stupidity.

I went to class and put the Loser List out of mind.

At lunch two hours later, there was an air of Something Going On. An extra-long line snaked around the juice machine into the hall. When I saw a piñata, my heart sank.

Mexican Day.

On theme days, there's always the danger of adults showing up in costume. Sure enough, Mr. Amundson, our desperately trying-to-be-cool vice principal, was dressed like a matador. I tried to avert my eyes but I was too late.

"What up, hombre?" he asked.

* MEXICAN DAY *

Pros:	Cons:

Salsa and chips

Cafeteria ladies in sombreros

Chili pepper lights

Hot sauce

Bean burritos

Bean burritos

"I'm fine," I said quickly, joining the lunch line. Reaching for a taco, I heard a girl's voice behind me.

"Hey, loser!" she said. Another girl laughed.

Who were they? I didn't dare look.

I quickly got in line at the condiments table. The girl ahead of me had a leather jacket and long, black hair. My palms began to sweat. Her back was turned, but I knew who it was.

Asia O'Neill.

What's so great about her? She's cool looking — long, dark hair and blue eyes. I don't always understand her clothes, but I like them. The stuff she carries hints at an interesting life: drumsticks, a skateboard, a graphic novel. She always looks slightly exasperated, which I take as a sign of intelligence.

And she is so, so out of my league.

* ASIA AT-A-GLANCE [NOT PICTURED]*

__Position__: Coolest girl in school

__Owns__: Paintball gun

__Accessory__: Zebra-striped skateboard

__Political affiliations__: Malibu Nussbaum for
  student council

__Hair smell__: Cherry Twizzlers

*I'm not a good enough artist to do her justice.
Sorry.

    I'm barely on her radar screen. In homeroom,
she's never turned around to compliment my
drawing of a skeleton or a pizza slice. I almost
never see her outside of class. The line moved
forward. As I squeezed the hot-sauce bottle, I
wondered what I could possibly say.

* BRILLIANT OPENING LINES:

    But before I could toss off one of these gems, Katelyn Ogleby shoved a taco under the dispenser. I knew her from class — an airhead who stuck to her best friend like a scented sticker. Sure enough, Ginnifer was next to her. They saw me and started whispering.

    "So, Danny." Katelyn's voice was mocking. "Who put you on the Loser List?"

"Geeks are okay," Ginnifer said. She's the nicer one. "It didn't say you were _psycho_."

"Well, _I_'d hate to be on that list," said Katelyn.

Asia walked by, reaching for a straw.

_NO_!

I couldn't let her hear I was on the Loser List! Panicking, I spun around to face Katelyn — but she was closer than I thought, and our trays collided. A splattered bystander jumped out of the way, and his salad went flying.

"FOOD FIGHT!" someone yelled.

The whole cafeteria went on red alert. A guy to my left fired the first official shot, throwing an open bag of tortilla chips. A burrito sailed by.

"_Un momento, por favor!_" Mr. Amundson shouted. But once the first burrito has been launched, little can be done to reverse it. In seconds, the fight was in full swing.

* FOOD FIGHT WEAPON CONVERSION CHART

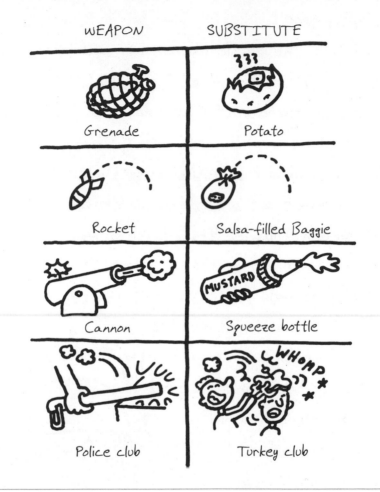

WEAPON	SUBSTITUTE
Grenade	Potato
Rocket	Salsa-filled Baggie
Cannon	Squeeze bottle
Police club	Turkey club

A guacamole missile struck Asia's leather jacket with a _thwop!_ She needed protection. Looking for a weapon, I realized I was standing next to the mother lode: five gallons of spicy goop.

I held the bottle like an Uzi and laid down some covering fire. A guy pointed a squeeze mustard bottle at Asia, and I blasted his whole head with red slime. He stopped and turned toward me, really slowly. Under the goop, I made out a studded wristband and Death Trawler T-shirt. My stomach dropped.

It was Axl.

I had just signed my own death warrant. Axl "Don't Call Me Morris" Ryan is the school's biggest bully, known for his do-rag, red face, and vacant

glare. He buzzed like an angry hornet and grabbed my collar.

"I — (gasp) —" My breath was cut off. Wristband studs pierced my neck as he choked me.

"How does that feel, punk?" he whispered.

"Hold it right there!"

Mr. Robinson, the school security guard, peeled Axl off me. Silence fell as Robinson scanned the room. Through narrowed eyes, he gave all of us his "You Are One Sorry Excuse for a Middle School" look. With his height and shiny bald head, he alone had the chops to stop the bloodbath. "Everybody sit down and finish your lunch. NOW."

He grabbed Axl's arm. "You're coming with me, son."

"WHAT?" Axl pointed at me. "It's his fault!" As Robinson dragged him away, he turned to me, dripping hot sauce. "You. Are. Dead. Meat." His angry blue eyes made my scalp freeze.

I gulped. Getting on Axl's bad side was a serious mistake. But Asia's gushing thanks would make it all worth it. "'S nothing," I'd say, as if defending beautiful girls was a routine event. When I headed back to her, she was picking corn kernels out of her hair.

That hair!

She turned to me with blazing eyes. "Thanks for starting a food fight," she said bitterly.

WHAT?

"This jacket is trashed," she said. "Are you happy?"

"Asia, I didn't —"

But she tossed her head and stormed off. I was stunned. On her behalf, I had just given Axl a hot-sauce facial! In the space of ten minutes, I had managed to antagonize the school's most attractive girl — and its most dangerous bully.

All because of that stupid Loser List.

I stomped back to our table. Jasper was reading, oblivious to the battle that had raged just inches from his head.

"You have taco meat in your hair." He turned a page.

"Jasper." I grabbed his shoulder. "We need to get off the Loser List. _Now._"

Jasper drained a juice box noisily.

"I'm serious. Girls are saying stuff. We need to go to the girls' bathroom and erase it. Today." I brought out the big guns. "If people think we're losers, you might not get sent to Quiz Bowl. It's by popular vote, remember?"

"Hmmm." Jasper frowned. Quiz Bowl was a contest for seventh-grade eggheads, and he was hot to go. "Interesting point. Can't we get someone to do it for us?"

"Who?" My voice squeaked. We slowly scanned the cafeteria, looking for any girl we knew well enough to ask. Out of 300 girls, there was . . . no one.

"I guess we're meeting after school," Jasper relented with a sigh.

"My locker," I said grimly. "15:30 hours."

Operation Bathroom Raid was on.

* CHAPTER TWO *

Jasper coached me at my locker. "The ability to move quickly and silently is our greatest weapon."

I rolled my eyes. He had been playing too much Ninja Master. While we waited after school for the halls to empty out, I rearranged my locker.

"Snake Fist." Jasper did a fake karate chop. "That's my ninja name."

"Right." I sorted through my junk. How had I collected so much stuff?

"Want me to scale a wall?" Jasper asked. "Shape-shift? Hey, that's my Viking hat."

"Hold on to your Nunchuks," I said, handing him the hat. "This is pretty straightforward. We go to the girls' bathroom, find the list, cross our names off. End of mission."

"Infiltration. Sabotage. Got it."

I'd seen that look in his eyes before. Like when he hacked into the school website to cancel classes on the opening day of _Avatar._ He loved having a daring plan.

We walked down the hall, blending in with kids racing to Cooking Club, Hooked on History, and other after-school activities.

Just our luck, we bumped into Mrs. Lacewell, who ran the school office like a military base.

"And where are you gentlemen headed?" She peered at us over her glasses.

Jasper blurted something about "after-school sports."

"Basketball?" Lacewell looked at Jasper's Viking hat and frowned. "Because that's the only practice going on today."

"Yeah." Jasper nodded.

Two big eighth-grade jocks in sweats came down the hall, bouncing a basketball and heading toward the gym.

"Uh, guys," Jasper called halfheartedly.
"Wait up."

The jocks looked back, laughed, and kept walking. Mrs. Lacewell narrowed her eyes. "Don't let me catch you sneaking into Dancercise. That's girls only."

"Nope. Basketball." I jumped up and tossed a crumpled napkin, missing the trash can. Lacewell "hmmphed," and we walked toward the gym. The second we were out of her sight, we raced upstairs.

Stepping into the door marked GIRLS was strangely thrilling. I wanted to look at everything. The tiles were pink, and the mirror was bigger than ours. I went over to look at a metal box in the first stall, but the words NAPKIN DISPOSAL made me back away fast.

I went back to the common area and scanned the graffiti above the sinks.

Pretty disappointing. I had secretly hoped it would look like this:

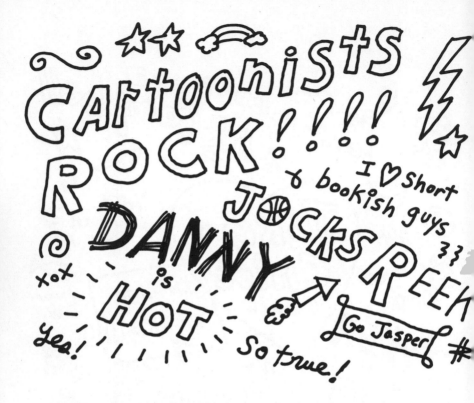

"Found it!" Jasper yelled from the last stall.

The Loser List — right. For a moment I'd forgotten why we were here.

My heart pounded as I switched places with Jasper. Sure enough, it was squeezed between JENNA + EMILY BFFS and KENDRA

Roxx. Next to each name was each supposed "crime."

* THE LOSER LIST

1. Barney Katz — BARFER
2. Jake Ogletree — WHINER
3. Saajid Dhurba — WEARS CLOGS WITH TUBE SOCKS
4. Luke Pringle — TALKS FUNNY
5. Dolf Gazzolo — ~~SYKO~~ ~~SYCHO~~ PSYCHO
6. Julian Kraft — HAS GIRL'S NAME
7. Ethan Fogerty — CANADIAN
8. Danny Shine & Jasper Koenig — BIGGEST ALL-TIME GEEKS

Ouch.

I felt liked I'd been socked in the stomach. What was the point of trying to impress girls with drawings? This was how at least one person saw me. If other people — Asia, for example — read the list, they might start to agree.

I had to cross my name out — fast. As I pulled the cap off my Sharpie, I heard someone cough.

"Ahem." Mrs. Lacewell was behind me. Her arms were folded, and she was peering over her glasses.

Waiting for an explanation.

"We just —" I looked around. Where was Jasper?

"Danny," Mrs. Lacewell said calmly. "What are you doing here?"

"My name's on this list." I dropped my pen. "See, I was just trying to —"

"Never mind, Danny." She shook her head. "I caught you red-handed, writing on school property. You gunning for the principal's office?"

"No, ma'am! I was . . ."

"Basketball practice." She ushered me out, snorting. "Don't think I fell for that."

Oh, man.

The principal was gone for the day, so we went to the assistant principal's office. The blinds were drawn, but the light was on.

"Mr. Amundson." Lacewell knocked on the door.

No answer.

"Mr. Amundson," she repeated.

Some shuffling, but still no answer.

"Mr. Amundson, this is an urgent matter."

Finally, Amundson's head peeked out. He looked extremely annoyed, and his hair was sitting on his head strangely. His toupee was one of the worst-kept secrets at our school.

* OTHER BADLY KEPT SECRETS:

1. Mexican Day leftovers get recycled into chili squares
2. Mr. Fingerroth doesn't read dates on hall passes
3. "we'll come back to that" means Ms. Lippert doesn't know the answer.

Mr. Amundson frowned. "Mrs. Lacewell, I am in the middle of important curriculum decisions. This is not the time —"

She burst into the office, dragging me behind her. From the stuff on Amundson's desk it was obvious what he'd been doing.

Mrs. Lacewell coughed, and Amundson's forehead turned red. He quickly shoved the clutter to the side of the desk and turned the mirror facedown.

"Yes, Mrs. Lacewell. What up?"

"Mr. Amundson, I found Danny in the girls' lavatory, writing on the wall with permanent marker. I'll leave you to discuss punishment." She forced me into a seat by pushing down on my shoulder.

The chair was lumpy and made my butt itch. "I was removing untrue graffiti, sir. That's why —"

"I don't give a rap why you were doing it."
Amundson tapped on the desk. "You were
defacing school property and that's NOT how I
roll." He liked to use kid lingo to show how cool
he was.

* AMUNDSON AT-A-GLANCE

Pet peeves: Under-the-
    desk gum wads, messy
    lockers
Resolution: Use "kickin'
    it" more in
    conversation
Prized possession: Fancy
    hairbrush
Quote: "Give it up for
    my man, Principal
    Kulbarsh."

"You know what this means," Amundson said gravely. "Detention — one week. Dissing school property — that's mad wrong."

A whole week! "But, sir, I —"

"You get props for good grades, Danny. But if you got away with it, what kind of example would that set?"

Oh, <u>man</u>. Detention was a nightmare — everyone said so. The hardened criminals of our school went there, and if I got thrown in with them for a whole week . . . ! What would I look like when they were done with me?

My heart began to pound. "Um — sorry about writing in the bathroom — honest. But is there anything short of detention I could —"

"No. Negative. Negatory."

Crud. I scratched my butt again, and realized I was sitting on something. Reaching under, I pulled up a mound of gray-brown fuzz. It took me a few seconds to register that it was another toupee.

I put it on the desk.

"What's...?" It took him a moment. "Give that to me!"

As he dove for it, his arm caught on an open jar. He looked down at his elbow, covered in pink gunk.

"Now look what you made me do!"

He opened the door, shaking with anger.

"Get...out...of...here," he said in a low voice. "Or I'll make it TWO weeks."

Jasper's jaw dropped. "No way."

  "Way," I said. "Starting Monday."

  Jasper's face turned white. We were at Comix Nation, our favorite hangout. I'd raced over looking for Jasper.

  "Oh, man." He covered his eyes with his hand.

  "How did you hide from Lacewell?" I asked. "She came in, and you disappeared!"

  "The toilet seat," said Jasper. "'Remain motionless like a stone' — an old ninja trick. I curled up so Lacewell couldn't see my feet." He shook his head. "Sorry she got you, though. Detention. WOW."

  He was starting to freak me out. "Jasper," I said. "Is it that bad?"

  "Those guys are animals," he said. "They'll eat you for lunch."

   "Geez, I —"

   "This is your last weekend of freedom."
Jasper shook his head sadly. "Try to enjoy it. Any
comic you want — Gossip Ghouls? Captain
Peculiar? It's on me."

   Now I was <u>truly</u> alarmed. Jasper was a total
cheapskate. He had read 200 issues of Rat
Girl — our favorite comic — standing in the store.

   "Hi, guys." Logan O'Brady, owner of Comix

Nation, walked by. She's a fierce comics snob, who scares young customers by rolling her eyes at stupid questions. We'd known her for three years, and liked to think we'd won her over. When she saw our faces, she stopped. "Did someone die, or something?"

* LOGAN AT-A-GLANCE:

Occupation: Comix
    Nation owner
Attitude: Surly
Makeup: Luke Skywalker
    lip balm
Pet peeve: Customers
    who read without
    buying.
Quote: "Hey! This ain't
    a library."

You looked better online.

"Not yet." Jasper coughed. "But — can you recommend something for Danny? I want to get him a present."

"You do?" Logan seemed suspicious. "How about this?" She unlocked the case under the counter. "Rat Girl, first edition."

The comic hit the counter. "Oooooh," we said, leaning closer.

"It's worth five hundred smackers," she said. "I can sell it if I ever go bankrupt. They'll have to carry me out first, though." It was the first time I'd seen Logan unlock the case. Only valuable first editions were kept there.

I whistled. I owned the 99-cent reissue — but this was the real thing.

"I'm trying to get Krazy Karl to stop here on his book tour," said Logan. He was the author of Rat Girl, and one of my all-time heroes. "We'll have a big book signing."

* MY FAVORITE RAT GIRL PRODUCTS *

"Well," Jasper said, "the first edition's nice, but . . ." He picked up a package of baseball bubble gum. "I'll take this instead."

"Big spender." Logan snorted and put Rat Girl back in the case. I heard the click as she locked it up.

"Thanks for the gift." I kicked Jasper. "Is that all I'm worth?"

"Nope." He threw some coins on the counter. "Gimme a jawbreaker too." He tossed me both packages.

Logan punched the cash register. "Thank God all customers aren't this cheap," she grumbled. "I'd be broke in ten minutes." Logan was her usual surly self, but I knew she only insulted people she liked. We were flattered to be treated like annoying younger brothers.

We wandered over to the dollar bins to look at back issues of Ooze magazine. The bell over the door jangled, and I heard footsteps. Jasper and I were arguing over The Blob's origin story, when I heard a girl's voice.

"Hi, Logan," she said. "Do you have the latest Shadow Grrrl?"

I looked up. It was Asia O'Neill!

"Hey, Asia." Logan directed her to the GIRLS KICK BUTT section. "It's over here."

My brain felt flooded. Asia O'Neill — in a comics store!

I shoved the magazine back in the bin, keeping my back to Asia at the cash register. Talking to her was out of the question. I pushed Jasper out the door.

"Bye, guys," Logan called out.

"Mmmphh," I muttered, pulling up my hood.

When we hit the sidewalk, Jasper said, "What's wrong?"

I'd never told Jasper about my crush on Asia. Who was I to even <u>think</u> about her? She probably wants someone who saves the rain forest, has an indoor climbing wall, and shaves.

* ASIA'S DREAM GUY *

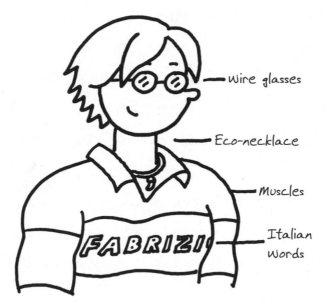

Wire glasses

Eco-necklace

Muscles

Italian Words

FABRIZI

I thought she was pretty cool before, but now that I'd seen her at Comix Nation...
She was off the freakin' charts!

"You have to admit," I dared to say to Jasper as we walked. "Seeing a girl that cute in a comics store..." I shook my head.

"I know." Jasper's voice was husky. "If I ever meet a female who knows the Green Lantern oath..."

We looked at each other and laughed.

* CHAPTER THREE *

I dreaded the end of classes on Monday. The final bell startled me — for once it seemed to come too soon.

Room 312 was known as "The Zoo," a dumping ground for GFMS's worst head cases, morons, and criminals. Walking over, I thought about Chantal's taunting, the food fight, the bathroom raid, and Amundson's office.

And after all that — I was still on the Loser List.

No one was there yet. The Zoo looked like an ordinary classroom — globe, pull-down map, calendar, pencil sharpener, and poster: CRIME DOESN'T PAY BUT A DIPLOMA DOES. I spotted an eraser torn in half, and a Snickers wrapper in the water cooler drain. Were those bloodstains on the desk?

Behind me, the door swung open. A group of guys burst in, talking loudly.

"...hamburger meat with ground-up rat in it. Everybody knows —"

I knew that voice. It was Axl. Of course he'd be at detention — maybe even because of the food fight I had started.

My palms began to sweat. When I turned around, Axl's jaw dropped.

"Holy —" he began. "You're the one who —"

I gulped. What could I say? Axl was probably here because of me.

We stared at each other. Him: studded wristband, greasy blond hair stuffed into a do-rag, and army jacket. Me: Acme Exterminators tee, video watch, and grandfather sweater.

* DETENTION: WHAT <u>NOT</u> TO WEAR *

Sweater Grandma knit

Fuzzy footwear

Math medal

This sign

"This guy really burns my butt," Axl announced to the other guys. Boris Lutz and Spike Jinwoo nodded. They all belonged to the Skulls, GF's only gang, the brains behind the School Statue Lingerie Show and the Fire Alarm Fake-Out.

* THE SKULLS *

Axl Ryan
Position: School thug
Likes: Skinny kids with lunch money

Boris Lutz
Ranking in Skulls: #2
Hobby: Fishing with a BB gun

Spike Jinwoo
Reputation: School's scariest Korean bully
Aspiration: To burn down a match factory

"He's friends with that dude in the cape," sneered Boris.

Jasper. I had to defend my friend. "He only wears it for special occasions."

"You're _both_ losers." Axl leaned close to me. "You know what happens to losers?"

An adult voice interrupted.

"New faces today." Mr. Gordimer dropped an overstuffed briefcase on the desk.

He was in charge?

My heart sank. Gordimer was the pale, puffy-faced wood shop teacher. He could teach you to build a spice rack, but couldn't control a class to save his life.

"Danny Shine," he read. "Boris Lutz. Spike Jinwoo. Morris Ryan."

Only adults dared call Axl by his real name, "Morris." Any kid who tried would be seriously disfigured.

"Luke Strohmer. Bruce Pekarsky," Gordimer continued. These were troublemakers at our school, guys I knew mostly from afar.

"Work sheets." Gordimer held up a stack of papers. "Pass 'em around."

A paper airplane sailed by, meant for me. Gordimer snorted and picked it off the desk. "Nice try, Ryan."

I sank into a seat and looked at my work sheet. The subject was "States and Capitals." Okay, whatever. I pulled out a pencil and started to fill in Harrisburg, Madison, Sacramento.

Behind me, there was giggling. A mechanical fart noise erupted, the kind that seeps from a whoopee cushion. Without looking up, Gordimer said, "Keep going, Ryan. That'll get you far."

<u>B-BOOM. B-BOOM. B-BOOM.</u>

Someone was banging a stapler on the desk. Between that and the fart noise, we had a real symphony going.

* MY FAVORITE SOUND EFFECTS *

Gordimer just kept reading his book.

"Strohmer, give it a rest."

Something hit me in the back of my neck. <u>Don't turn around</u>, I told myself.

<u>Ow!</u> Something hit my shoulder.

It was getting harder to — <u>WHAP!</u> — ignore. I slowly rotated my neck and <u>THUNK!</u> — direct hit. The crowd cheered. Axl and his gang were shooting spitwads, and their aim was impressive.

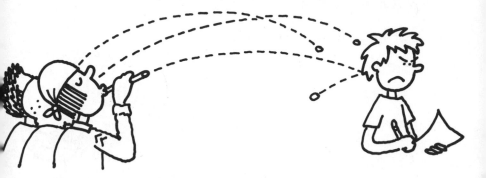

PLINK! A rogue spitwad beaned Gordimer on the ear.

He swatted it like an insect. "What in Sam Hill...?" he muttered. After another — DING! — hit him on the forehead, he finally put down his book. "Cut the horseplay!"

Something blue and green shot across the floor. I recognized the globe zooming by. Luke had lifted it off its base, and kicked it like a soccer ball. PLONK! It hit Gordimer's desk.

The globe bounced off the file cabinet and hurtled back in a high arc toward Gordimer's head.

That pushed him over the edge.

"YOU WANT TO STAY ALL NIGHT?" he roared, standing up. "I can stay all night." Now globe soccer and the fart symphony were happening simultaneously. Gordimer

dove after the globe, trying to catch it before anyone could kick it again. He corralled it and shoved it under his desk.

Axl leaned over to my desk. "I want to ask you something, Loser. You started that food fight, so how come I got blamed for it?" He made my desk shake. "Huh?"

I leaned back to display my work sheet, in

case he wanted to copy it. But Axl didn't take the bait. "Why don't I just walk you home later?" he asked.

Crud.

"Walk you home" was code for "maim beyond all recognition."

* POSSIBLE RESPONSES:

"Sorry, I have karate class."
"My fight calendar's completely booked."
"No need — my dad picks me up in his squad car."

* ACTUAL RESPONSE:

"I, uh, can't after school. I'm busy . . ."

Axl's eyes opened wider. "Doing WHAT? Going lipstick shopping?"

The bell rang, and I ran.

"Get him!" Boris shouted.

I shot out of detention like a rocket. At the chain-link fence near the soccer field, I bent to catch my breath. No one was around except some girls twirling batons.

Phew!

I'd outrun Axl, or else he'd stopped to beat up someone else. I let out a huge sigh of relief.

"Hey, Loser."

Axl and his crew stepped out from behind a tree. My stomach took a dive.

How had they gotten ahead of me?

Crud.

Double crud.

"Time for our walk," said Axl. He dumped his backpack, while Boris grabbed my arms from behind. Taking off his army jacket, Axl rubbed his knuckles. My heart was pounding like crazy.

So this is what it's like to get beaten up, I thought.

Axl rolled up his shirtsleeves, showing a slice of homemade Sharpie tattoo. In spite of my terror, the artist in me was curious. Did Axl draw it himself? I stretched to get a better look.

"Could I, uh, see your tattoo?" I said.

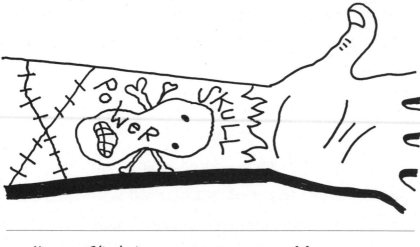

"What?" Axl seemed thrown off.

I pointed to his arm with my chin.

"Oh, for God's sake." He scowled but let me look at it.

I tried to twist out of Boris's grip. "Who did it?"

"Who cares?" Axl spat on the ground.

He pulled back his arm again. Before he could punch me, I blurted, "You know, I could draw you one a million times better."

"WHAT?" He sounded angrier than ever.

"Something really cool and unique, something that's, you know, worthy of the Skulls." Put the arm down, I prayed.

Silence.

"Really?" Axl's eyes darted around.

"He's yankin' your chain," grunted Boris. "Let's ice this guy and get it over with."

Axl pulled his arm back, and I shut my eyes. Seconds later, I realized Axl still hadn't hit me, and I opened them again. "So." He rubbed his fist. "Uh, what would you draw?" he asked.

58

My stomach flip-flopped. Was this actually working?

"I'll...show...you." I said, struggling out of Boris's clutch. "Let me get my backpack." I pulled out my sketchbook and showed him my greatest hits.

"That's not all," I said. "I kind of, like, specialize in violent, bloody, horror stuff."

"Yeah?" He sounded interested.

I skimmed the book quickly for something that would make his mouth water.

Axl licked his lips, possibly picturing it inked across his bicep.

"Not bad," he said to Spike and Boris. "Could you do a really cool skull or a twisted, bloody heart with a knife in it?"

Yes!

"No problem," I said.

* CHAPTER FOUR *

The next day, detention rocked.

"Can you make the flames look hotter?" Axl asked while I worked on his arm. Boris, Spike, Luke, and Bruce ("Bruiser") watched with fierce concentration. Work sheets titled KNOW YOUR PRESIDENTS sat on our desks, untouched.

Today's supervisor was Mrs. Wagman, a friendly English teacher with big glasses. Aside from the occasional "Language, people!" she left us alone. Everyone was quietly

absorbed, watching the skateboarding skull come alive on Axl's forearm.

"How do you get the brains to spill out like that?" asked Bruiser.

"Add motion lines." I showed them how to draw maggots and cracked skulls. After I put the finishing touches on Axl's arm, he stretched it out to show everyone. More _ooohs_ and _ahhhs_.

"That is so rude." Axl flexed his arm. "Thanks, man."

"You do graffiti?" Spike spoke for the first time.

"Sure." Actually, I didn't. I worked in pen, not spray paint.

"I want to write 'Skate or Die' on the halfpipe," he said. "Can you show me some rad lettering?"

"Well, Spike." I felt my voice get deeper. They were treating me like an expert! "I'd probably do something like . . ."

I was showing
off, knowing Spike
wouldn't be able to
copy me. But I tore
the page out of my
sketchbook and
handed it to him.
   "Cool. Thanks,"
he said. 
   I showed them
other things to draw.

SKATE OR DIE

Zombies

Garbage

Explosions

They showed me their doodles too. "Nice,"
I said, looking at Bruiser's barbed-wire border. I

showed Luke where his bloody knife could use shading. I put stink marks on Spike's barfing alien. And of course, I got more requests for tattoos.

"Flaming motorcycle!"

"Gangsta robot!"

"Slime freak!"

When the bell rang, no one moved. I was finishing a snake on Bruiser's arm, while my audience watched, fascinated.

Finally, Wagman kicked us out. "It was nice to see everyone so absorbed in their work sheets," she said.

When we hit the hall, Axl gave me a friendly shoulder-chop. "You're all right, man."

Ow — that hurt. "I'm glad —"

"No, really." Suddenly, I was his great pal. "Normally, I don't like . . ." He searched for the right word ". . . dweebs. But you did me a solid, and I don't forget that."

"Oh, well . . ." Better than getting beaten to a pulp.

"So what are you in for?"

Writing on the girls' bathroom wall didn't sound tough enough. "Uh — breaking and entering, and — entering and breaking. How about . . . ?" I stopped, remembering the food fight.

"Listen," Axl said. "I'm all about payback. What can we do for you? TP a house? Prank calls? Swipe something?"

Huh. Yesterday I was roadkill — now he was dying to do me a favor.

"Got anybody you need threatened? Swirlies, skirt floats, Mexican wedgies?" Like a waiter naming the specials.

Then it hit me.

"You know," I said. "Actually, there _is_ something..."

Watching Axl sneak into the girls' bathroom felt good. Finally, the job was being handled by a pro.

Boris stood guard like a bored nightclub bouncer, while I hung out nearby. It was passing period, and Axl had barricaded himself inside the bathroom. Angry girls crowded around, banging on the door.

Axl poked his head out. "Danny, _where's_ the list?"

"Last stall," I whispered.

66

He disappeared inside.

"What is he _doing_?" cried some girl. "I need to go."

"I'm getting the principal!" someone else shouted.

Oh, boy.

Axl reappeared, motioning for me to come in. I hesitated — could I risk getting caught? He pulled me inside by my sweatshirt. "Show me," he said. "Quick."

I slammed the door shut and brought him to the stall. "There it is." I pointed. "Next to 'Corbin is a dipwad.'"

He read the list with disgust. "This is stupid," he muttered. Good — we agreed. "Fogerty should be ranked, like, second or third," he said.

So much for solidarity.

"Just take my name off," I said. "And Jasper's."

"On it."

I went and held the door closed while people pounded on it. Axl came out of the stall to grab a paper bag with something metal in it. He went back in. I heard a furious scraping noise and then — thud. Was he removing the plumbing too?

"Done," he called out.

I peered into the stall. My name was gone, and so was a chunk of the wall. A pile of cinder-block chips sat on the floor. I was stunned; I had assumed he'd cross it out with a marker. "Good, huh?" he asked, holding up a crowbar.

"You didn't need to..." I began, but thought better of it. "Never mind."

THE LOSER LIST
1. uum
2. awm
3. uum
4. uum
5. u

Jenna M

If Amundson thought I'd defaced school property <u>before</u>, what would he think now that we'd destroyed a wall? I dumped the cinder-block heap in a trash can.

Then I heard Chantal's voice outside. "Whoever's in there is gonna get seriously beat up —"

"Let's go," I begged.

"Yeah," Axl said. "Gimme a pen. I want to add something."

AXL is **Hot**

Even <u>he</u> wanted to put in a good word for himself.

Looking around for something to cover my

face, I saw Axl's paper bag. Perfect! I pulled it over my head and hid behind the door.

Then I opened it.

Shouting girls swarmed in like an angry hive. Before I could escape, someone plucked the bag off me.

"Danny!" It was Chantal. "Get your sorry butt outta here!"

"I —"

"What are you even doing — ?" Then it hit her. "The Loser List!"

"It's gone," Axl said. "I wasted it."

She spun around and saw him. "What?" she demanded. "You know each other?" Chantal seemed surprised. She and Axl were known enemies.

"Yup." Axl wiped off his crowbar. "Part of the list is still there. Not Danny's name, though."

The two of them were attracting a crowd primed for a Battle of the Bullies.

"Then I'll just write it again." Chantal stuck her chin out. "And add your name."

"No, you won't." Axl mopped his brow. "Cuz if a Loser List goes up with Danny's name on it . . ."

I stepped up and whispered in his ear. "Or Jasper's," he added, "you're gonna have to deal with me."

Chantal laughed. "SO? I'm not scared of you!"

Axl had on his if-you-weren't-a-girl-I'd-demolish-you look.

"Don't bait me, Chantal," he said grimly. "Or that milk carton bird feeder you made is toast."

Chantal's face went pale. "You can't go in the display case," she gasped. Everyone knew how proud Chantal was of her eco-project showcased outside the principal's office.

"Oh, yeah?" Axl smiled. "Try me."

She narrowed her eyes and swallowed. "You are one sorry lowlife."

"Ooooh." The crowd turned to Axl. Now that I wasn't the target, I could enjoy the drama — sort of.

"Fair warning." Axl shrugged.

Boris came up to us and gave Chantal a heavy-lidded stare. "You got trouble?" he asked Axl.

"Naaah," said Axl. "Let's go."

The three of us hurried down the hall while I mumbled some appreciative words.

My name was off the list — at least for now. Maybe Chantal would leave me alone. I stood up straighter and threw my shoulders back.

Knowing tough guys was kind of . . . useful.

"Don't worry about another list going up," said Axl. He fist-bumped Spike and Boris. "We'll take care of Chantal."

I laughed uneasily, wondering what "take care of" meant.

* CHAPTER FIVE *

The next day I moved through the hallway feeling ten pounds lighter. My two biggest problems — Axl and Chantal — hated each other more than me. Through the crowd I spotted Axl's blue do-rag, and wondered if he had different ones for special occasions.

I made a beeline to ask him if he'd gotten in trouble for the bathroom break-in. Our forbidden activities secretly thrilled me. Why did

I have to be Mr. Never-Do-Anything-Wrong?
Maybe it was time to live more dangerously.

   Axl was leaning against a locker, bumping fists
with someone. I moved closer to see who it was.

   Asia!

BUMP

   Axl and Asia together — I couldn't believe it.
Was Axl her type? Seeing Asia whisper in his ear
made my stomach churn. It rearranged my
picture of her: Maybe she was one of those girls
who wore eyeliner to gym and hung out in the
school parking lot after school.

Un-tucking my shirt, I vowed to be tougher in the future.

* "BAD BOY" CHECKLIST *

I got to them just as they were splitting apart. "Hi!" I called out to Asia as she veered into the crowd. My eyes must have followed her, because Axl elbowed me.

"Hey," he said. "Don't slobber." I felt my face get hot.

Chantal spotted us from across the hall. "Hope you're enjoying detention!"

Actually, it was the highlight of my day. I missed hanging out with Jasper, but I liked playing

Art Genius and helping the guys draw pictures of Rakim the Rotten or a skeleton on a motorcyle. And of course, I drew more evil Sharpie tattoos:

I also got strange requests. Boris thought the girl in the anti-choking poster needed a mustache. Luke wanted the banner on his heart-shaped tattoo changed from "Luke & Fiona" changed to "Luke & Amber." Bruiser asked me to forge a note.

"I started one," he said. "But my handwriting reeks."

PLEASE EXCUSE BRUCE FOR MISSING SCHOOL TUESDAY. HE WAS HOME

WITH THE FLEW, NOT AT FRANK'S
FUNLAND.
SINCERLY,
MRS. PEKARSKY

I corrected his spelling and handed it back.
"Lose Frank's Funland," I ordered.
Bruiser blinked. "Oh. Okay."
In fact, detention was becoming so
weirdly enjoyable I tried to get Jasper
to come.
"It's kind of a goof," I said. "Can't you
commit some cyber crime, or something? Hack
into the teachers' website! That'd get you in
trouble." He had dropped by my place after I
got home from detention. As usual, he was glued
to a video game.
"What?" He vaporized some Zarks. "You said
it was a death sentence."
"Yeah, but it's better now," I said.

Jasper was silent a moment. "You only like it 'cuz those guys ask you to draw skulls on their arms. What would I do?"

"Show 'em science experiments," I suggested. "They like blowing stuff up."

"Pass."

"But —"

"Danny, they're a bunch of thugs," Jasper insisted. "Why are you hanging out with them?"

I paused. His question hung in the air.

"We're not hanging out." But the truth was, I'd miss detention when it was over. Being with the Skulls was like studying another species. Their minds worked in strange and amazing ways. What would it be like to just do what you wanted, without worrying about teachers or parents or getting in trouble?

And now there was — hard to admit — the Asia Factor.

Ever since I'd seen her and Axl fist-bump, I kept replaying it in my head. If Asia liked tough guys, it didn't hurt to keep on the Skulls' good side. But I wasn't going to say that to Jasper.

"I get a kick out of 'em." I shrugged. "That's all."

But I was careful not to mention my next drawing "job."

*   *   *

Axl had asked me to draw on the "Wall of Fame" in front of the refurbished gym. Recently painted pure, snowy white, it was reserved for displaying newspaper clippings about the Fighting Woodchucks soaring to victory. So far this year, we hadn't won anything to brag about.

Explorers see a mountain and want to climb it. Axl sees a wall and wants to deface it. As we walked out of detention, he described his vision. "'Skulls Rule' in creepy lettering," he said. "Like out of a horror movie."

"Not the award area," I said quickly. "It's too new." Something about the dumb hopefulness of that wall got to me.

"No, definitely there," he insisted. "It's perfect."

Before I could refuse, he pulled out a pack of matches. "I want lettering like this."

The lettering was cool. But I stood firm. "No, Axl. Sorry. Do it yourself if you want it so bad." I picked up my backpack, hoping

that would be the end of it.

Axl's eyebrows drew together. "Do it myself?" Drawing his own graffiti struck him as crazy. "It'll look like garbage."

I shrugged.

"C'mon, help me out," he went on, practically begging. "If you do, I'll —" I watched him try to think of something. "I know!" He put on a low, singsong voice. "I'll put in a good word about you with Asia."

Hearing her name made my chest squirm. Just a little.

No. No. No.

"C'mon, man." He could see he'd hit on something. "I'll tell her you're cool next time I see her. That she should get to know you."

Really?

My brain felt flooded by chemical responses. Not a good time to think about the smell of her hair —

I stuffed the matchbook in my pocket and walked away.

"Tomorrow morning," Axl called after me. "I'll meet you there. Seven thirty sharp."

On the way home, I cursed myself. Why had I agreed to draw on school property? What was I thinking? I didn't want to ruin the new space. Axl had a way of getting people to do stuff. And this time he hadn't even threatened to beat me up.

I slept badly, thinking about what I'd agreed to do. The next morning I made it to school early, but Axl was nowhere to be found.

I headed over to the gym to look at the wall. Blindingly white. Begging for graffiti.

Might as well get it over with. First I looked both ways down the hall — empty. I reached for my jumbo marker like it was a hand grenade. I pulled the cap off with my teeth, like a grenade pin, and started to draw.

SKULLS RULE

"Danny??"

I jumped ten inches. When I whipped around, I saw Jasper standing next to me with his backpack. Since when did he lurk around gym before school started? My stomach sank.

"Geez." I wiped my brow. "You scared me."

"Coach Kilshaw wanted me to look at his computer." He stared at my drawing. "What's this?"

"No big deal." I felt embarrassed. "A favor to Axl."

Something changed in Jasper's face.

"Axl?!"

I tried for sympathy. "Stupid — I know. I got roped into it. I should've just . . ." I couldn't even finish the sentence.

Silence.

Then Jasper shook his head. "You don't do stuff like this. What's going on?"

"Oh, please." I rolled my eyes. "It's a stupid drawing."

"Those guys are using you," he said, and he sounded really angry. "Can't you see what's happening?"

"Jasper." My voice was shaking. "I did him a favor. Big deal. Now just <u>back off</u>."

"It's like I don't even know you anymore," said Jasper. "What's next — setting a locker on fire?"

Talk about overreacting! But his words sank to the pit of my stomach.

"Jasper, you've got it totally wrong —"

We heard footsteps, and froze. Axl appeared, out of breath.

Lousy timing.

"Awesome." He looked at the graffiti. "You really came through — it's like you're a Skull already. By the way, can I have my matches back?"

At that moment, I couldn't look at Jasper.

"Don't come over this weekend," he said, and walked away.

Axl slapped me on the back.

"Great," he said. "You can hang with us."

* CHAPTER SIX *

"What do you wanna do?"

"I dunno. What do you wanna do?"

It was the world's oldest conversation, but on Saturday afternoon, it felt new — I was having it with Axl, Boris, and Spike. After my fight with Jasper left me alone all weekend, Axl talked me into joining them. I knew I'd regret it, but some combination of loneliness and curiosity pushed me over the edge.

The four of us were parked in Axl's bedroom. Intimidating rappers and long-haired guitar gods stared down at me from posters. And instead of books, the shelves on every wall held . . .

Sneakers.

Rows and rows of them, in different fabrics, colors, shapes — with straps, stitching, and logos. They all looked brand-new. Axl saw me staring at them.

"Didn't know I was such a sneakerhead, huh?" He chuckled.

"Not really."

"But you saw my vintage Nike Terminators..."

Had I? All sneakers looked the same to me. "I didn't know you were, uh, into sports. Do you wear them all?"

Axl sniffed. "They're not for wearing."

"He collects 'em," Boris said.

Axl pulled on a thin glove, like he was handling rare Chinese porcelain. He picked up a high-top. "See this? Laser-etched design. Only sold in Asia." He moved to another shoe. "Glitter panel on midsole."

Axl was a nerd, I realized. As detail obsessed as any D&D fan. It made me like him more.

"If you could have any shoe you wanted —" I started to ask.

"White-on-white Air Force Ones in anaconda skin," he answered automatically. "Killa Whale wears them." He pointed to a poster of an enormously fat rapper wearing two gold watches on one wrist.

He took out another shoe. "Want to touch it?"

I reached for it, and he pulled it back again.

"Wash your hands first." He pointed to the bathroom.

When I got back, he handed it to me. "The NBA didn't allow the original version of this shoe. Violated uniform rules. Michael Jordan was fined five thousand dollars every time he wore them."

"Wow."

"True story," Axl said.

I handed the shoe back, and he wiped it down with a toothbrush. When he left to get more cleaning fluid, I looked at Boris, who was sullenly staring at the wall. I asked if he collected anything.

"Street signs," he said.

"Which ones?"

"Any ones."

Axl came back. "Okay, guys — what are we going to do today?"

I didn't want to throw out the first idea.

Spike sat up. "Set off cherry bombs?"

"Waste snakes with dart guns," said Boris.

"Spit at people from the overpass," Axl said. "Knock over bikes. Been there, done that, bought the T-shirt. Let's do something different today.

Danny —" He turned to me. "What do _you_ do for fun?"

   "Well it, uh, depends..." When Jasper and I hung out we mostly just talked, but that didn't seem manly enough. I thought about what else we did.

   Thinking about his lumpy couch, I felt a stab of longing, but then stopped myself.

"Go to movies, buy comics," I said. "Stuff like that."

"Comics, huh? Where?"

"Comix Nation," I said. "Downtown, next to Just T-shirts. The owner and I are friends." Pride crept into my voice when I mentioned Logan.

"Friends with the owner?" Axl sounded impressed. "Really?"

"Sure." As much as a twelve-year-old guy could be friends with a stuck-up forty-year-old female comic book geek.

"Let's go," Axl demanded, jumping up. "I need some air."

"How about Funland?" asked Spike.

"No," said Axl. "We're going to the comics store."

I was sorry I'd mentioned it. What if we ran into Jasper? Looking at Axl's shelves, it didn't seem like he was into reading. Well — if he wanted to look at comics and graphic novels, I couldn't stop him.

Besides, once Axl made up his mind, he didn't change it.

On the walk there, Axl pointed out certain places of interest. "This is where I beat up Skippy Lipowicz." When we passed the hockey stadium, he said, "Jonah Stuhl wrecked his bike here." He showed me an intersection where he once saw a three-car pileup, and pointed out graffiti he admired.

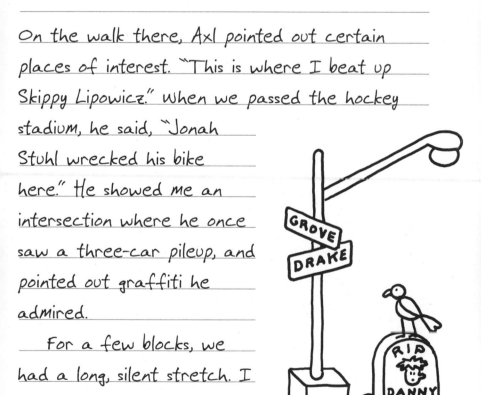

For a few blocks, we had a long, silent stretch. I guess no one had been beaten up on that street.

How long till they would be showing people where I got demolished?

I tried to make conversation too. "What are you guys, uh, doing this summer?"

Axl snorted. "Summer school." Wow — he knew already?

* TOP THREE SIGNS YOU'RE GOING TO SUMMER SCHOOL

1. You flunked lunch.
2. No one buys you a beach pass.
3. On the last day of school, Amundson says, "See you Monday."

Axl asked about my summer plans. "Computer graphics camp," I said. "Probably."

"Can I ask you something?" Axl studied me. "When did you become such a geek? Were you, like, born that way?"

His tone wasn't hostile, just curious. I realized Axl found me every bit as unusual as I found him. Maybe everything we said to each other boiled down to one basic question: <u>How did you get to be so different from me?</u>

"I'm not a geek." Explaining this over and over was a drag.

Spike nudged me. "Do you know what 'http' means?"

"Yeah."

"You're a geek."

We finally arrived at Comix Nation. Spike opened the door and started to go in, but Axl pushed me in front. "Danny goes first," he said sharply.

Being a VIP had its perks.

The first thing that always hits me at Comix

Nation is the smell: old comic books mixed with bean burrito, or whatever take-out food Logan was snarfing down. I loved this place.

As usual, Logan was parked at the cash register.

"Hey." She thrust out her hand. "Gimme some skin."

"Hey," I replied, and slapped her palm.

I reached down to pet Logan's dog, General Zod, named after a Superman villain. Axl's gang disappeared into the comics racks. "Where's your partner in crime?" asked Logan.

Thinking about Jasper made me wince. "He's not here."

"Duh." Logan snorted. "What's the matter? I thought you guys had a Vulcan mind meld."

"I dunno." I kept looking into Zod's bleary eyes.

* GENERAL ZOD AT-A-GLANCE:

Occupation: Dog

Resides: Under "Japanese Bootlegs A-F"

Size: Huge

MEET
KRAZY KARL
CREATOR OF
RAT GIRL
COMIX NATION
4 PM NOV 6

"Guess what?" Logan's face lit up. "Remember I told you I was trying to get Krazy Karl here? Well, he's doing it. Here's the poster."

Krazy Karl — whoa! I read the poster excitedly. On Friday, he was coming to Comix Nation for an "Artist Talk" and signing. Great! I wondered if Jasper had heard.

"Think you'll get a big crowd?" I asked.

"I hope," Logan said. "There's not much time to spread the word. The people I've told are pretty psyched."

As one of the few female comics store owners, Logan strongly promoted Rat Girl and other female comics heroes.

But that was the only thing girlish about her. When guys talked down to her, she loved to shock them by spewing details about Dr. Vile's lab, or dropping Magneto's original name. She knew more about comics than anybody, girl or guy.

Where were Axl and the crew? I stretched my neck out, and spotted them checking out a Super Vixen calendar. "New friends?" Logan asked in a low voice.

"Oh." I tried to sound dismissive. "Just — guys I know."

"They don't seem like your type," she said.

I shrugged. "They're okay."

"Hey!" She tugged my sleeve. "Want to see what I got at Comic-Con? It's in the back room."

The back room!

That was like getting on Air Force One, or back stage at Madison Square Garden. It was rumored to house a rare copy of Stinky the

Bat #1, and a secret dungeon for people who
confused Star Trek and Stargate.

  I followed her into a cavern with a sign
that read, KEEP OUT! THAT MEANS YOU! I
almost tripped over a bright red beanbag chair
next to an old-fashioned Super Mario machine.
A pizza box on coffee cans served as a
coffee table.

Stacks of unsold comics spilled out of Hefty bags. "I guess Vomitron never took off," I said, peeking in.

"I can't even give those away." Logan sighed. "But check out this swag." She pulled a two-headed bobble-head anime weasel out of a Flash Gordon bag. "And look — a toaster that burns a Batman stencil into your bread."

"Oh, man." I couldn't wait to tell Jasper — until I remembered for the hundredth time we weren't speaking.

When Logan and I returned to the front of the store, the guys were looking through baseball cards.

"We're leaving," Axl said. He sounded bored. I was about to tell the gang to go on to Funland without me. But before I could speak, Axl gripped my shoulder and pushed me out. As we left, Logan handed me a flyer for Krazy Karl's reading.

"Be there." She looked at me pointedly. "I'm counting on you." Nodding, I stuffed the paper in my backpack.

When we hit the street, Axl turned around.

"Okay, guys: whadja get?" he asked.

I stiffened — when had they bought something? Axl pulled a comic out from under his shirt, and I saw the Rat Girl logo.

My throat tightened.

"Did you . . ." I gasped. "Buy those?"

The diamond stud in his ear winked at me. "You kidding?" Axl smiled. "I <u>hate</u> paying for stuff."

I felt like someone had punched my lights out.

* CHAPTER SEVEN *

"Are you out of your mind?" I sputtered. My heart was pounding so hard I could barely hear myself think. "Logan's my friend!"

Axl and Boris high-fived. "I know," he said. "That was excellent. You kept her gabbing so long, we could have cleaned out the store."

What?

"Axl." My voice was dead serious. "Take these back. Or I swear, I'm telling Logan myself."

Axl stopped in front of an empty bus shelter and motioned for us all to sit down. Spike and Boris slumped on the bench, but I shook my head.

"Danny, Danny, Danny. You're not telling Logan anything. You know what happens to snitches?"

Spike and Boris jumped up to surround me. Axl grabbed my jacket collar and Boris rolled up his sleeves. Spike caught my elbow and twisted it.

"Owwwwww." It felt like he was tearing my arm off.

"You think _that_ hurts?" Axl laughed. "That's nothin.'"

Intense waves of pain shot through me as Spike twisted even harder.

"Tell 'im what we did to Ethan Fogerty," said Boris.

Axl and Spike snickered.

I could only imagine.

I yelped some more, and Axl nodded for Spike to stop.

He released me, and I fell back, clutching my elbow. Pain radiated up my arm, even though he'd let go. Had he broken it?

"You're with us," Axl said. "So if you tell anyone, you'll only be ratting yourself out."

"What does that mean?"

Axl shook his head. "We did this <u>together</u>. You knew what would happen if we went."

"No, I didn't!"

"You should have." Axl rolled his eyes. "What did you think I was there for — baseball cards? I've got to get extra scratch where I can. Collecting sneakers ain't cheap, you know."

I wanted to run away. But I had to get the comics back to Logan somehow. For now, I'd have to pretend to go along with the game — or at least assure Axl I wouldn't rat the Skulls out.

Rubbing my arm, I took a deep breath.

"Hey," I said, "sorry about the freak-out. The Logan thing threw me, that's all." I took another breath. "I won't tell. But could I just — see Rat Girl?" Maybe I could trick Axl into lending it to me so I could return it to the store.

"Okay." Axl sounded relieved. "I didn't think you were that stupid." He motioned for Boris to hand it over.

Whoa.

It was issue #1!

My jaw dropped.

"It was locked up, so I knew it was worth something," said Axl.

Five hundred smackers, according to Logan. I can sell it if I ever go bankrupt, she had said.

How had they opened the locked case?

As if reading my mind, Axl added, "That lock is a joke. All I had to do was jimmy it with my ID card."

My mind tried to take this in. Stealing issue #1 took everything to a whole new level.

"Can I see the others?" I asked.

Boris handed over two ordinary comics taken from the rack — nothing valuable.

I tried to sound casual as I asked, "Are you going to sell this? I know guys who'd buy it. If I took it home, I could —"

"No way." Axl snatched it out of my hand.

"I'm bored," whined Spike. "Now can we go to Funland?"

We started walking to the video arcade. Axl slapped me on the back. "Glad you came to your senses," he said. "Cuz I think with your geek image and our muscle, we could really go places."

Boris looked skeptical. "Maybe."

"He's the perfect front man," Axl argued. "He has that Mathlete look no one suspects." He turned to me. "Don't worry, we'd give you a cut. We could go to Value Barn, Music Town, anywhere."

In spite of everything, the word "Mathlete" stung.

"And if you prove yourself, you could..." Axl's voice trailed off. "Not definitely, but there's a chance — become a Skull yourself. With the blood initiation and all."

"Me... join the Skulls?"

"It's every guy's dream." Axl sighed. "I know."

For a second, I tried to imagine myself as a Skull.

We finally arrived at Funland, a deafening video arcade bulging with kids. At the door I tried again.

"Hey, Axl." My tone was lazy. "Could I just take Rat Girl overnight? I never read this one." That was a lie. I'd read the reissue dozens of times.

"Nope." Axl frowned. "You coming in?"

This was my chance to lose them. "No, I — gotta get home."

"Great day, man." Axl offered his hand for a fist-bump.

Great day?

It had been, maybe, the worst day of my entire life. As Axl smiled, I imagined Logan's face when she looked in the glass case. Had she discovered Rat Girl was missing yet?

She'd be cursing like crazy, sorry she'd ever let us in. And today, of all days, when she'd invited me into the "No One Allowed Here — EVER" back room! Her good-bye played over and over in my head.

"I'm counting on you, Danny."

I felt like I was going to vomit.

* CHAPTER EIGHT *

All I had to do now was steal a high-ticket item from a pack of professional thieves.

No problem.

Once I got hold of the comic, I'd go to the store and replace it while no one was looking. That way, no one would get in trouble. I could only imagine what the Skulls would do if I ratted them out.

Lunchtime was the magic hour, I decided.

That was when Axl & Co. shook people down for lunch money. First they dumped their backpacks, and then hit the lunch line for victims. While they were busy, I'd grab Axl's backpack, and replace Rat Girl #1 with my 99-cent reissue. After school, I'd take the real comic back to Logan's store.

It was good to have a plan.

The next day, I brought the reissue to school. I was nervous all morning, tripping over a hockey stick in gym, flubbing a social studies quiz. By the time I hit the cafeteria for lunch, my heart was pounding.

At least I had something to do. Lunchtime hadn't been fun lately, without Jasper. I missed the days when we'd spend the hour arguing about what would be the worst way to die.

We usually sat at the Tech Geeks' table, but since our fight, I didn't feel welcome there. Scanning the room, I saw an opening at Sixth-Grade Airheads. Perfect: no one would talk to me, and I could keep my eye on the bullies.

* GF CAFETERIA *

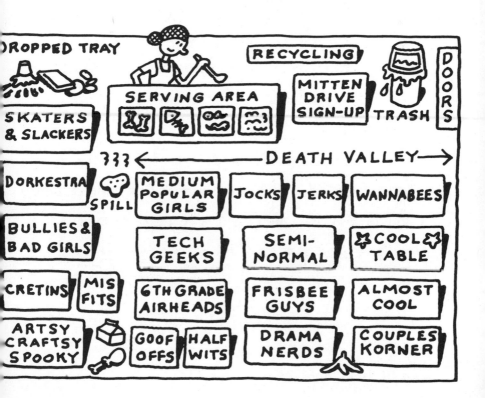

I took out an old Planet Zorg comic, hiding the Rat Girl reissue underneath. When the Lunch Money Roundup began, I'd spring into action. Sure enough, Axl's posse dropped their stuff in a heap at Bullies & Bad Girls. Usually, you weren't allowed to "save" a table, but who was going to tell Axl?

The guys rolled by the lunch line like a six-legged monster. They moved into position at the base of Death Valley, where innocent bystanders had to pass on the way to the steam table.

I held my breath, watching Axl's every move.

He taunted a few sixth graders, and tripped a kid in khakis. Impatient for real action, I silently begged him to find someone — anyone! Finally, he and Boris closed in on a guy with a calculator on his hip. They were facing away from me.

It was now or never.

Like a crazed Delta Force commando, I pounced on Axl's backpack. I quickly pawed through his junk, ignoring stares from nearby tables.

No comic.

Did Boris or Spike have it? I peeked in the dirty pillowcase Boris carried as a book bag.

Then I checked Spike's drawstring pouch.

I glanced back at Axl — now pelting his victim with pita chips, while Boris twisted his arm.

If they could hold him just a _second_ longer . . .

I dove into Axl's bag again, this time noticing side flaps. Excitedly, I reached into one — empty. The other held a potato chip bag. Stuffing it back into the pouch, I felt something stiff. Reaching in, I pulled out Rat Girl #1.

Yes!

I sighed with relief, but cursed the chip bag. This was a first edition — he could show some respect. The guy cleaned sneakers with a toothbrush, but treated a valuable comic like dirt.

I eased the #1 out of its plastic, and slid the reissue in to replace it. I hurried away from the table, keeping my eyes peeled for Axl.

Where was he? Lunch line, tables, trash bins? No —

Coming right at me.

Had he seen me steal Rat Girl? Should I act like nothing happened or run like crazy? I veered casually away from him, but he jumped in front of me. "What were you doing?" he asked, pointing to his backpack.

"Needed a pen." I tried to smile. Should I run?

Axl handed me a ballpoint.

"Here," he said. "I got plenty."

Perversely, his reaction made me sad. Axl actually _trusted_ me.

"Thanks!" I grabbed the pen and turned to run, dropping some stuff from my backpack.

"Wait." Axl bent over. "Is this yours?" He waved a yellow paper.

"Keep it!" I yelled, sprinting for the door.

* CHAPTER NINE *

The minute school let out, I flew to Comix Nation. Rat Girl #1 was hidden in my bag. The big question was, had Logan noticed it was missing?

To avoid ratting on anyone, I'd slip the comic back into the glass case. When Logan was away from the counter, I'd jimmy the lock with my ID card — just like Axl had described. To do the right thing, I had to become a thief myself.

Pathetic.

When I got to the store, I saw things not usually seen at Comix Nation.

Cars   Crowds   Girls

What was going on?

As I got closer, I saw a poster taped to the window. Of course! It was the day of Krazy Karl's book signing! I'd been looking forward to this. How could I forget?

What rotten luck.

Now I'd be breaking into a locked

case in a room of fifty people. Should I come back the next day? But then it hit me: Logan would probably open the case at the end of the reading, so Krazy Karl could sign that valuable first edition.

The clock was ticking.

There was also a chance of running into Jasper. That would be bad. If he ignored me, I'd be bummed out. And if we did talk, how would I explain what I was doing? I remembered the last time I saw him. "It's like I don't even know you anymore," he'd said.

I felt my stomach twist.

When I opened the door, the place was packed. People were sitting everywhere — on folding chairs, comics price guides, boxes.

All eyes were on the gray-haired man at the metal table.

Krazy Karl!

He was older than I'd imagined. Like someone's grandfather, maybe, but with a mad gleam in his eyes. He was stroking a large parrot, bright green with splashes of yellow and red near its beak.

Across the room, my eyes met Logan's — the moment I'd feared. For a split second, her face was blank. But then she broke into a smile. "Isn't this cool?" she mouthed. "All these people!"

Phew.

She must not have noticed the missing comic.

I edged toward the locked case, which was behind the audience and across the room from Krazy Karl. I wanted to be in position before the reading started.

"'Scuse me." I stepped around a girl in a WHAT WOULD RAT GIRL DO? T-shirt. "Sorry."

"Watch it," someone said.

Finally, I got up to the case — only to find a fat guy in black high-tops sitting on it.

"Could you, uh, move your leg?" I asked him.

He moved his giant knee half an inch.

"More?" I waited.

Scowling, he slid another inch — enough so I could see through the glass. The shelf looked like it always had. I could see a Rat Girl title, partially covered by another comic.

If you looked close, you could see it was another issue — Rat Girl #7: <u>Tails from the Crypt</u>. Like any good shoplifter, Axl had rearranged the shelf so it looked the same. That was why Logan hadn't noticed.

I needed to get behind the counter. The locked case could only be opened from the back. On the way, I knocked over a stack of baseball cards. Thwap! They scattered, giving me an excuse to crawl behind the case.

"Idiot." High-Tops Guy snorted.

I inched around the back of the counter. The room was still noisy, so I had to work fast —

"Quiet, everyone!" Logan yelled.

The room fell silent, except for one loud squawk from the parrot. Now every sound would be extra noticeable.

Logan stood at the front of the room. "From the Golden Age of Comics, the creator of Rat Girl, Terriblo, and Derek the Dog. A brilliant artist, mangler of young minds, and truly twisted individual. This guy is the real deal. Put your hands together for . . . Kra-a-a-a-zy Karl!"

I tried the latch on the case — locked. I reached for my school ID card.

Everyone cheered as Karl waved. "Thanks, Logan. Jennie and I are happy to be here."

Karl pointed to the bird on his shoulder. More cheers, and then the room fell silent again.

I inserted the card in the lock.

"What are you doing?" A girl stretched her neck over the counter.

I looked up, panicked.

"Picking up baseball cards," I whispered.

"You missed one." She pointed.

"Oh — thanks." Fake smile.

She turned back around.

"I'd like to read from Issue number 178," Karl said. "Rat Girl: <u>Rodent of Steel</u>. Here, Sarah Bellum sends an asteroid hurtling toward earth..."

* MY FAVORITE RAT GIRL SUPER VILLAINS:

The Exterminator

Sarah Bellum

The Human Worm

I slid my ID card back and forth, trying to find the release lever in the lock.

"In her secret command center high atop the Ashikagi mountains..."

Back and forth. Back and forth —

"Sarah Bellum stood in front of a brain-wave scanner..."

Back and forth. Back and forth —

"'Rat Girl's days are numbered,' she said."

Back and forth. Did I feel something?

"'Using mind control, I'll...'"

YESSSS! The lock released! I slid open the glass —

"'...erase her personality...'"

Now all I had to do was slip in the comic, relock the case, tiptoe out and —

"Need some help?" I felt a hand on my shoulder.

It was Axl.

* CHAPTER TEN *

Holy crud! Did he follow me here? How had he...?

Axl held up the yellow paper I'd dropped in the cafeteria — a flyer for the reading! Karl was near the end of the story. Soon, Logan would come over to the case and —

"Walk away," Axl whispered. He was crouched beside me behind the counter. "Now."

High-Tops Guy looked over. "S-h-h-h-h."

"Now," Axl repeated.

"No." My firmness surprised me. "No freakin' way. I'm putting it back. That way no one gets in trouble."

"No?" Axl sounded shocked. "It's mine!"

"It's hers!" I hissed back.

"Zip it," said High-Tops more sharply.

    I stretched my neck up over the counter. People were staring. "Don't be stupid," I whispered. "Or we'll both —"

    Axl stood up and grabbed my shoulder. His other hand was balled into a fist. "Listen, dirt bag —" Axl's voice got louder, and he raised his fist above his head.

    "Quiet!"

    "Give it!"

    "Shhhhhh!" Too late — the whole audience turned around. Krazy Karl stopped reading.

    "Hey!" Logan stood up. "Get away from that counter!" She pointed at Axl. "No one's allowed there!"

The crowd buzzed.

"Me??" Axl acted outraged. "I'm trying to help. He's the one stealing!" I thought I was going to keel over. Suddenly, he stood up and lifted me by my jacket.

"Ooooooh," everyone murmured.

Logan squinted. "Danny?"

Axl turned to me. "Go on. Show her."

"Please." Logan snorted. "Danny would never . . ."

"He's a thief." Axl's voice was confident. "Check his backpack."

Oh, no. No, no, no, no, no.

"Check his backpack," Axl insisted.

Was this really happening?

Nobody moved.

"Okay, I'll do it." Axl lunged at me.

I backed away, colliding with a stack of action figures. Ka-flump! They tumbled to the floor. As I collapsed in a heap of plastic, a guy in a baseball cap

reached down and

grabbed my backpack. I

was numb with dread.

"Open it," said Axl.

Baseball Cap Guy

rummaged around for a

second, then held up

Rat Girl.

"Oh my God!"

someone yelled. "That's

issue number one!"

Everybody gasped.

Logan was dumbfounded. "Danny???" The crowd started to boo and hiss. Someone threw a spiral notebook at me. An empty water bottle hit me in the shoulder, then a pack of gum. This was unreal.

"I can explain!" I begged. "It's not what you —"

A juice box struck me in the chest.

Through the booing, I heard the front door jangle. Axl had left the building.

* CHAPTER ELEVEN *

"I'm gobsmacked," said Logan. "Just — gobsmacked."

I wasn't sure what that meant, but I knew it wasn't good. The audience was thrilled. I felt sick to my stomach.

"Logan." I tried to steady my voice. "Here's what happened: Last week when we came in, Axl stole the comic. When I found out, I stole it back from him. I was just returning it!"

For a moment, she looked torn.

"I'd never steal from you." My voice was low. "Ever."

"Nice try!" someone yelled. "But the comic was in his backpack!"

Logan looked uncertain. The crowd started to boo.

"I saw him picking the lock!" a girl volunteered.

"Me too!" said someone else.

"GUILTY! GUILTY!" the crowd chanted.

"I was just putting the comic back," I insisted, my voice hoarse.

"GUILTY! GUILTY!" The chant grew louder.

Logan opened her mouth, like she was about to ask me something — and then changed her mind. "Yeah, right." She glared at me. "And then you were abducted by aliens. How stupid do you think I am, Danny?"

Everyone snickered. "Don't let the door hit you on the way out," she added. My body felt paralyzed. "_Now!_" In a daze, I floated toward the door.

I'd take alien abduction over this _any_ day.

Suddenly, Krazy Karl stood up. "_I'd like to say something._"

Everyone stopped talking.

"Young man." His watery blue eyes met mine. "You have shamed yourself before these great fans of graphic storytelling," he thundered. "You've betrayed Logan, a nurturer of creative minds. You have scoffed at us who use art to fight boredom and make sense of a baffling world."

"Karl," I pleaded. "No! You've got it wrong — totally. This is a huge mistake —"

I'm one of you guys, I was trying to say. I use art to fight boredom and make sense of the world! That's how I survive! I use art every day ...

To get through school

Kill time

Make friends

Appease enemies

No one loved comics more than me. I couldn't live without them!

Karl turned to the audience. "Let this be a lesson to you all. Does anyone know what Rat Girl does to shoplifters?"

Voices called out.

"Feeds 'em to sharks!"

"Throws 'em in a volcano!"

"Disintegrates 'em!"

I got the idea. Letting Logan down was bad enough, and knowing Jasper would hear about it was excruciating. But being publicly declared a world-class creep by your all-time hero . . . ?

That was devastating.

Logan held open the door for me. "You're banned from the store." Her lip was trembling. "I should call your parents, and the police."

"Logan, you don't —" I was frantic.

"Game over, Danny." Logan's voice rose.

Oh, God. "But —"

"I'm done with you." Logan rubbed her temples.

"GUILTY! GUILTY!" The chanting started up again.

"Can't we go somewhere and talk?" I whispered frantically. "By ourselves?"

"No." Logan's voice was shaky. "Get out."

Reluctantly, I staggered outside. When I

passed in front of her, she turned her eyes away. "Geez, Danny!" she burst out. Her face puckered strangely, like she was trying not to cry.

Had I actually brought Logan to tears? Tough, seen-it-all Logan? The woman who bullied

customers for not knowing Lizard Lady's middle name? The fan girl known as "Logan the Destroyer"? That was like making Rat Girl cry.

I hit the sidewalk, trying to take it all in. At least Jasper hadn't shown up. He hadn't seen me go down in flames. If Logan actually called my parents, or the police... I shuddered. It was bad enough thinking about all the things I wouldn't be doing with her anymore.

    I was deep in thought, when something shot out of the bushes.

    "AYYY-YAHHH!"

With a wild kung fu yell, my attacker threw
me to the ground. When I opened my eyes, I
was flat on my back on the lawn beside the
Pancake House. Axl was leaning over me with
his arms planted on either side of my head.

"Wassup?" He stared down at me.

I blinked, and tried to sit up. Axl pushed me back down. The new worst day of my life had just gotten a little worse.

"What do you want?" I said.

"Just a friendly warning." Axl's face was right above mine. "If you snitch..." He wiped his nose with the sleeve of his army jacket. "You're a dead man. Got it?"

"Unh." I tried to nod.

"I'm serious," Axl said. "Wasted, whacked, six feet under. Worm food, zombie zone, Last Exit to Brooklyn."

I groaned.

"You breathe one word about us stealing the comic, and — oh, man. We've got things in mind for you we haven't tried out on anyone. Stuff out of James Bond."

I nodded again.

"As it is, you're in big trouble." Axl's head loomed over me. "Already. For taking that first edition out of my backpack." His eyes narrowed. "I found out what it's worth."

My voice was weary. "It belongs to Logan, Axl. How'd you feel if someone swiped your first-edition LeBrons?"

"You're ungrateful." Axl waved his hand. "You got to hang with the Skulls, man. It doesn't get better than that. And you abused the privilege."

He actually sounded hurt. He loosened his grip and rolled off of me. I got to my feet and ran out to the street.

"If you snitch, you're dead!" Axl roared.

I didn't look back.

* CHAPTER TWELVE *

At school the next day, everyone was buzzing about the crime. A few people frowned at me, and Katelyn Ogleby hissed, "Shoplifter!" I caught sight of Jasper in the hall, but he was still avoiding me.

Ty Daniels gave me a puzzled look. Fiona Sterry-Eckstut switched seats so she wouldn't have to sit next to me.

I wasn't exactly captain of the football team <u>before</u>. But now I'd probably sunk even lower on the food chain.

ME

At lunch, I parked myself at Misfits. I figured I belonged there. But when Pinky Shroeder started distributing photocopies of his butt, I had decided I was better off completely alone. I spotted a bench under the air conditioner.

I was moving to the bench when Chantal called me over.

"Danny!" She patted the bench next to her. "Plant your sorry self right here." Reluctantly, I sat down at Bullies & Bad Girls. "What's this crazy talk 'bout you stealing a five-hundred-dollar comic book?"

"Um, it's a long —"

"Give it to me straight up." The whole table leaned in to listen.

Tough position. If I told the truth, Axl would get me for ratting them out. I looked at the Skulls, at the other end of the table. Boris saluted. I was already on Axl's bad side. If I told what really happened, who knew what he'd do?

Did I have to just suck it up?

"It was him!" Brady Spitzer pointed at me. "Randy Furman saw it!"

Some of the girls giggled.

Chantal turned to me and raised an eyebrow dramatically. "Is it _true_?"

The table got quiet. I leaned forward, not sure what I'd say. THWAP! A French fry beaned me on the nose. "Sorry," Axl said. Our eyes met for a moment, across the table. I turned to Chantal —

And nodded.

"Really?" Her voice rose. "You're not playing?"

I shook my head.

"DANG. I mean, you're such a geek and all." There was something new in her voice. Was it . . . respect?

A crowd had started to gather.

"How'd you get into the locked case?"

"Did you break the glass?"

"Where'd you hide it?"

There must have been at least twenty people there. At GF, it usually took a bigger event to draw a crowd.

Fight

Lost retainer hunt

Public barfing

Now people at other tables were drifting over. A couple of cute girls from the Medium

Popular table stopped by, and I saw Axl stare at them. "Do you ever _pay_ for comics?" one of the girls asked me.

"Hey, Lucy." Axl pushed me out of the way. "You should see the stuff _I_ do." I had to laugh — it was like _he_ wanted the attention! On the very edge of the mob, I saw a slice of purple cape.

Jasper.

He stood there clutching a backpack the size of a small refrigerator. His mouth was tight and his face looked pale. His body was only half turned toward me, but I could tell he was listening.

I suddenly lost my appetite for public speaking. Once again, fear of Axl had stopped me from telling the truth. That's why I was in this mess —

because I hadn't had the guts to go to Logan in the first place. It was probably too late, but I had to come clean to someone.

"Gotta go," I announced to the crowd. As they dispersed, I followed Jasper through the lunchroom. It's hard to go after someone who hates your guts, but I had to try. I took a deep breath and tapped him on the shoulder.

"Can we talk?"

Jasper spun around. My throat went dry.

"I don't think so," he said. His eyes flashed with anger.

"Just hear me out." My voice was quiet. "If you don't believe me, we never have to talk again. One conversation: that's all."

"I'm busy." His voice was just as quiet. But he didn't move.

"Ten minutes." I said.

"No."

"Jasper," I pleaded. "Come on."

"NO!" Jasper took off his science safety goggles, and we had a staring contest. I tried not to blink. "Oh, for God's sake," he said finally. "Just make it _fast_."

We ducked outside and sat on a concrete bench. I had one shot to get it right.

I swallowed, and then told him the truth about the Great Rat Girl Heist. Jasper put his goggles back on and leaned in. As honestly and straightforwardly as I could, I described every tragic mistake.

1. I hung out with Axl & Co.

2. Talked to Logan while Axl stole the comic.

3. Stole it back.

4. Tried to return it.

5. Got busted.

Jasper listened. I watched for a reaction, but it was hard to see his eyes through the goggles. He nodded his head, and said, "Oh, man," at different points. When I finished, neither of us spoke for a few moments.

Then Jasper shook his head.

"Danny." He sounded like he was trying to control his anger. "You were incredibly stupid."

"I know," I said. "If I'd been able to talk to you about everything..." I looked at the ground. He'd have known what to do. "Now it's too late."

"Yeah. Well."

"I can't believe Logan didn't believe me," I said.

"You can't blame her," Jasper said. "All she saw was —"

"Hey, Danny." Luke Strohmer tapped my shoulder. "Will you get me Alien Smackdown IV? I heard you get five-finger discounts."

"Beat it," I snapped.

"Selfish," whined Luke.

I turned back to Jasper. "You see what I'm dealing with?" My voice broke. "Some of these morons are actually _impressed_. I thought Axl was going to have a cow. He wished _he_ could get the credit."

"Yeah?"

"He got this look." I snickered. "Like he was jealous, or something."

"Really?" Jasper said. "That's interesting."

"Yeah. Some cute girls were asking me questions, and he started bugging out," I said. "He was dying to set them straight."

"That's it!" Jasper blurted out.

"What?"

"That's how you prove you didn't do it. Get Axl to rat himself out."

"Huh?"

"It's simple." Jasper's voice rose. "Make the theft sound so awesome, he won't be able to let you take credit."

I saw the old gleam in Jasper's eyes. He loved an against-all-odds fight. "We just need to build up how brilliant and fearless you were..."

Did he just say "we"?

"You'll have to work fast," he said. "Right now, everyone's interested, but by next week they'll be talking about something else."

GF had a short attention span.

"Meet me at the office after sixth period," said Jasper.

Yes!

* CHAPTER THIRTEEN *

"The office" was the janitor's supply closet, which we treated like a private conference room. We were under the gun because Ralph, the janitor, could show up any moment.

I'd ditched study hall that afternoon to meet Jasper. Now I was trying to get comfortable on a giant drum of sawdust, the kind you spread on vomit.

"Here's what we do," said Jasper. "We get Axl and his gang in a room with people they'd like to impress. And by people, I mean —"

"Girls."

"You brag about stealing the comic. Axl sets the record straight. I get the whole thing on tape. We send it to Logan," he said. "Simple."

"Which girls?" I asked.

"The one with the fur jacket," said Jasper. "Who's friends with the one with big hair. And the other one."

Jade Traxler, Kiki DeFranco, and Angie Bilandic — names known by every guy at GF, except Jasper. A trio of shallow, pretty girls who wore lots of makeup, cut classes, and always looked too dressed up for school. Not vying for the Science Prize, but very cute. Axl would be keen to impress them.

Kiki DeFranco
Reputation: Tough-
talkin' mall rat
Diet soda intake:
Hefty

Jade Traxler
Reputation: Boy
crazy
Likes: Mustaches,
motor scooters

Angie Bilandic
Reputation: Dim bulb
Lives for: Pajama Day

"Where do we do it?" I asked.

"The media room," said Jasper. "It has recording equipment. When you start to brag, Axl will interrupt. I'll record what he says. Bada-bing, bada-boom."

"How do we get them there?"

"Leave that to me," Jasper said. "First we need to find blank tapes. The media room's so old, they still use cassettes."

I heard the squeak of a bucket wheeling down the hall.

"Hi, fellas." Ralph was back. "What can I do you for?"

Ralph was part-time; the rest of the week, he tried to get work as an actor. Sometimes he asked me to run lines. As a district attorney or medieval friar, he wasn't bad — janitor was the only role that didn't suit him.

"Chalk," I blurted. "Mrs. Lugar's all out."

"Hmmm." Ralph stroked his chin. "Now, where would that be?"

He started pulling random boxes off the shelves, and tossing them in a pile. "Paper clips — no, that's not it." The supply room floor was a mess. "Staples. Where the heck — ?"

CRASH!

"Dagnabit!" Ralph looked at the pile of glass at his feet. "Lost another box of beakers."

"Any good acting jobs lately?" I asked.

"Organic food commercial," said Ralph. "Good money, but — the costume gets really hot."

"Now, where's the chalk?" Ralph put down the broom, and started pulling out boxes again. Every time he

brought one down, he'd read the label and
shake his head. Jasper and I pretended to help,
hoping a box of cassettes would turn up.

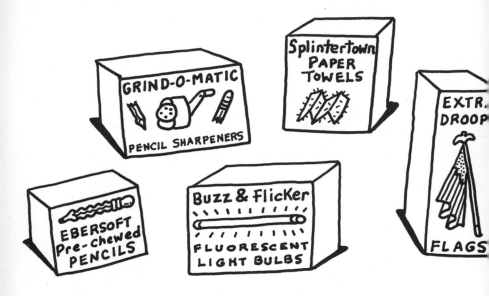

"Danny!" Jasper whispered. In the corner,
he'd discovered an electronics graveyard, with
dusty VCRs, film projectors, and a turntable.
We'd hit pay dirt. I saw Jasper pull out a
cassette tape.

Suddenly, the first few notes of a song from the musical _Wicked_ rang out, and Ralph dropped another box.

"Whoops!" He dove for his phone, and lifted it to his ear.

"My agent," he mouthed. "Come back later?"

While Ralph was yakking, Jasper slipped the tape into his backpack.

We waved to Ralph and hurried out the big metal door.

* CHAPTER FOURTEEN *

"I've got to de-frizz my hair, so this meeting better be fast."

Kiki dumped her purse on the desk. It was the size of a toaster oven, with complicated buckles and pouches.

All seven of us were in the Media Room, seated at desks in a circle — Jade, Kiki, Angie, Axl, Spike, and Boris. The room was a recording studio, where morning announcements were made over the PA system. The walls were soundproofed to keep out noise from the halls.

In the corner was a control booth, with a big glass window. Jasper was in there, tinkering with the dials.

"This is the Fashion and Celebrity Gossip Club?" Kiki frowned. "I thought it would be, like, all girls."

"Fashion?" Axl jumped up. "My flyer said, 'Violent Video Games Focus Group.'"

Everyone started talking at once. "They told us we'd get paid for testing —" "It said we'd be modeling —"

"Guys! Guys!" I held my hand up. "There are a couple of different meetings. Wait till the leaders get here."

Axl sat down slowly, letting his eyes linger on Jade, who was applying berry-colored lip gloss. Spike and Boris were throwing chewed gum at the wall. I knew I couldn't hold them for long.

"What's he doing there?" Kiki noticed Jasper in the booth.

"Fixing equipment," I said, waving dismissively at Jasper. "Ignore him."

I glanced nervously at a box on the floor. It was filled with electronics junk and spare parts — but if you looked closely, there was also a microphone sticking out. We'd covered the floor with cables, so you couldn't see the cord that reached from the microphone into the control booth.

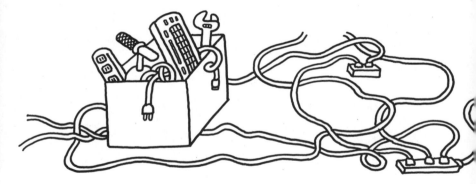

Only Jasper and I knew that the mike was on.

"Hey, Danny." Angie cocked her head. "I heard you were kicked out of school for stealing." The girls leaned in. "What happened?"

Axl's head snapped up.

"What'd you steal?" Kiki sounded skeptical.

"A comic book," I said casually. "First edition. Worth five hundred dollars."

"Will you go to jail?" Angie's eyes were shining.

"Ooooh," said Jade.

"Or the juvenile work farm?" Angie seemed excited.

"What happened when the police came?" Jade's voice was breathless.

Axl shifted in his chair.

Wow — I didn't have to exaggerate. These girls were doing it for me. The myth around me had grown huge. Jasper looked at me from the glass booth and suppressed a smile.

"I don't buy it." Kiki's eyes narrowed. "You're not the criminal type."

"Well..." I pulled my arms back into a lazy stretch. "Guess you don't know me very well."

Boris and Axl exchanged glances.

"Aren't you like — kind of a geek?" Kiki pressed.

"Dunno." I lifted my chin. "Do geeks break into stores and steal first-edition comic books?"

"Huh." Kiki considered this. "How long have you been stealing?"

Axl cleared his throat.

"How long have I been alive?" I was starting to enjoy this.

Angie's eyes got bigger and rounder. "Don't you worry about — the danger?"

"Danger?" I snorted. "I laugh at danger."

I glanced over at Jasper, who rolled his eyes. Axl opened his mouth, but then snapped it shut again.

A rush of power swept over me — three cute girls were hanging on my every word! When had that ever happened?

Axl cleared his throat. "Ahem."

Everyone ignored him.

"Ahem."

"Shhhh, Axl." Jade kept her eyes on me. "Danny's talking."

Axl made a strangled sound.

"Tell us about it," said Jade. "From the beginning."

"Aaaaaaaaaaarrrrrrrrrrgh!"

Everyone turned to look at Axl. He was howling like an enraged bear. Smoke was practically shooting out of his nostrils, and his face was the color of corned beef.

"NOTHING!" Axl exploded. "He did NOOOOTHIIIIIING!!! THE GUY IS A TOTAL LIAR! I STOLE THE COMIC, NOT HIM! THAT'S WHAT I DO!"

The other guys looked alarmed.

"Axl!" Boris whispered.

Things were working out perfectly.

I held my breath as Axl buried himself, slowly and clearly. "I. Stole. The. Comic. Get it? Not this pathetic loser art geek."

SCORE!

BINGO!

HOME RUN!

I glanced over at Jasper, eager for his thumbs-up. But Jasper didn't look thrilled — in fact, he looked completely panic-stricken. Why was he waving his arms like that?

"Excuse me, guys —" I bolted over to the booth.

Jasper pulled me in and slammed the door. Looking down, I saw the tape had stopped.

"The recorder's busted," Jasper said hoarsely. "It got stuck and tore the tape." He lifted up a broken strand.

"What?"

This was beyond disastrous. I looked around frantically. Nothing but the control panel for —

"The PA system," I blurted out.

"Huh?" Jasper squeaked.

"Put it over the PA." My voice was tense. "It's our only option." I pulled out the cable connected to the microphone and plugged it into an auxiliary port on the control board.

"Are you crazy? It'll play over every speaker in school. Axl will kill you!"

"He won't hear it in there," I said. "It's soundproofed."

"Yeah, but —" Jasper frowned. "You <u>sure you</u> want to?"

Of course I wasn't.

But at least I could clear my name at school. And who knew, maybe word would get to Logan. It was super risky, but I had to try.

"He's not tough! He didn't do —" In the other room, Axl was still ranting.

It was now or never —

"— squat! I'm the one who —"

I cued Jasper to flip the switch.

Busting out of the control booth, I raced back to my seat. No one noticed the "on air" light had turned green. As Axl strutted around, Boris rubbed his temples, and Spike fidgeted with his jacket zipper.

The girls looked flustered.

"I opened the stupid" — Axl stopped for breath — "comics case. I'm a pro! Danny didn't even know we did it." If you listened really, really hard, you could hear the faintest trace of the loudspeakers in the other classrooms.

Axl kept talking. "He's never done anything like that. Danny hangs out in the girls' bathroom. His mom labels his underwear!"

The whole school was hearing this. I imagined six hundred people laughing.

what other secrets could he reveal...?

Axl was clearly enjoying himself. "He wears no-name sneakers like my grandmother! And the biggest joke is: he thinks he has a chance with Asia O'Neill!"

My face felt like it was burning up.

"He loooves her." Axl laughed. "Pathetic!"

I stared at the floor. This was large-scale, public humiliation.

Broadcast schoolwide.

"His only friends are giant geeks." Axl snorted. "Like this guy Jasper —" He pointed to the glass booth.

Even in my sorry state, I couldn't let that go by.

"Um, Axl?" I stood up.

He ignored me. "Talk about a humongous loser. This guy —"

"Axl?" I stopped in front of him.

"What do you want, freak?"

My voice was calm. "Jasper is the coolest guy I know. He has more brains in his left tibia than you have in your whole Neanderthal body. He's light-years ahead of everyone at this school. Girls go crazy for him."

"Tibia . . . ?" Boris frowned.

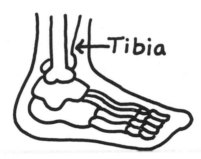

In the control booth, I could see Jasper mouthing, "Girls?"

"Look it up," I said. "In ten years, Jasper'll be famous. He'll have invented a DNA notebook, video transmogrifier, or orbital digitron. He's got ideas to burn, off-the-wall interests, and a wicked sense of humor. Who wouldn't want him as a friend?"

"But he's a geek," Axl scoffed.

"There are worse things." I shrugged.

Axl seemed taken aback.

"About the comic." I turned to the girls. "Axl's telling the truth — I didn't steal it; he did. Stupidly, I tried to return it to the store without telling anyone. The owner caught me opening the case and — the rest is history. Right, Axl?"

"Right." He sounded less certain. "Told you he didn't have the guts."

"It's true," I agreed.

Axl looked confused. What fun was it to trash me if I agreed with him?

"For the record, I didn't get expelled or forced to work on a chain gang," I said. "No police. What I did was plain and simple stupidity. Starting with who I chose to hang out with."

I looked over at Jasper. This last point was for him. My way of admitting what an idiot I was.

"Well, now I don't know who to believe," Jade pouted.

"You don't <u>know</u>!" Axl was frantic. "Who do you think sets off fire alarms at this school? And lets air out of teachers' tires?"

Boris turned to Spike. "Get him out."

The guys grabbed Axl by each arm. "Who TP'd the principal's house? Trashed the welcome sign? Gave the school statue" — they were dragging Axl out the door — "<u>women's underwear</u>???"

They were gone. No one spoke for a moment.

Within seconds, Axl would learn he had been heard by the whole school. I tried to catch Jasper's eye. Bolting might not be a bad idea.

"Well, that was exciting." Jade's face was flushed.

We heard pounding at the door. A crowd was piled outside, trying to peek in. Through the window, I could see people pointing and giggling.

"Geez." Angie looked at the clock. "Is this stupid meeting ever going to start?"

* CHAPTER FIFTEEN *

I motioned to Jasper. "Take the back exit."
We left the girls and ran out the back, down
the side hall, then hurled ourselves into the
empty photocopy room. When the door shut, we
started yelling.

"Can you believe it?" he whooped.

"Axl fell for it! Totally!"

"Did you see his face?"

"Wait till he realizes —" I began, but
stopped.

I was still in trouble.

When Axl found out his confession had been
broadcast in every classroom, hall, and office at
school, he wasn't going to be happy. In fact,
he'd be furious —

Beyond furious.

I'd wanted him to brag about stealing comics, but he'd gone way beyond that — ranting about fire alarms, and TP-ing the principal. Now his disaster was _my_ disaster. If he got seriously punished, what would he do to me?

Yeesh.

Even aside from Axl, I had big problems.

I still needed to get straight with Logan, and deal with everyone else at school. I had gone from being ignored to publicly humiliated.

The thought of facing Asia after what Axl had said made my head throb.

"Sorry about the recording mess." Jasper's cheeks turned crimson. "I'm glad we — sort of — had a backup."

"'S okay." I tried not to sound disappointed. "I just hope Logan hears about it."

"I couldn't believe how over-the-top you were," Jasper said. "'Danger? I laugh at danger!' You laid it on a little thick."

"Probably," I admitted. "It was fun. Part of me hated to come clean." It was nice getting teased by Jasper again.

"The stuff you said about me . . ." Jasper's voice trailed off.

We both looked at the ground, embarrassed.

"I've got to run. Um . . ." Jasper hauled his backpack up. "Tomorrow night is mud wrestling on cable. Helga the Huge vs. She-Wolf."

"Yeah?" I looked at him carefully. Did that mean...?

"Yeah." He shrugged. "Be there at eight."

"'Kay." Yes.

I opened the door, deeply relieved. Now I could face everyone else.

When I got to the main hall, people ran up to me.

"OMG!" One girl squealed. "That broadcast was hilarious! Does your mom really label your underwear?"

"So, you're crushing on Asia!" another girl said.

They dissolved into giggles.

Not a good sign. I worried the takeaway from Axl's rant was Danny is a wimp who thinks he deserves the coolest girl at school.

"What's in the girls' bathroom?" Luke Strohmer asked, smiling.

I walked away, sneaking into an empty stairwell to plot my next move. How could I get to Earth Science without being noticed? Pulling up my sweatshirt hood, I drew the drawstrings tight so only my nose stuck out. It covered my face, but made it hard to see.

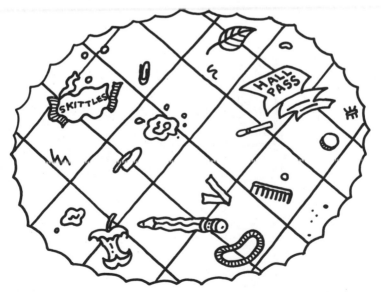

"Danny?"

Through my sweatshirt hood, I heard a girl's voice. If I walked fast, maybe it would go away.

"DANNY!"

Someone tugged at my sleeve. Through my hoodie hole, I saw a terrifying sight.

Asia O'Neill's feet.

Crud.

My impossible crush had just been trumpeted to the entire school, along with details of my loser-ness. And now, I had to run in to her.

So much for my "tough" act.

"Hey," Asia said. "Could you put the hood down? I want to talk."

Pretending not to hear, I kept walking.

"I'm <u>happy</u> it was Axl who stole the comic," she said loudly, "and not you."

That made me stop. I turned around.

"Those guys are bad news," she said. "I'm glad you're not one of them."

"Really?" I tilted my head back to see her from under my hood.

"Take that stupid hood down!" she ordered.

I pulled it off my head. My hair was probably sticking up like a lunatic's. She looked cool, with layered T-shirts, and GI dog tags around her neck. "I thought you and Axl were friends," I said.

"Why did you think that?"

The day couldn't really get more humiliating, so I kept going. "Last week you were talking in front of the water fountain." I sounded like a second grader.

BUMP

Asia burst out laughing.

"Are you kidding?" she cried. "I tutor him in math. I was congratulating him for getting a D-plus instead of an F."

Oh.

She was Axl's <u>tutor</u> — not his friend! My chest suddenly felt lighter. But then I remembered Axl ranting, "He thinks he has a chance with Asia O'Neill!" and felt like sinking into the floor.

I had to say something.

"Uh, Asia." I couldn't look at her. "When Axl, um, said that thing about . . ."

"Yeah?"

"Me, thinking I had a chance with . . ." I stumbled. "You know, you —"

"Forget it," Asia said with a wave of her hand.

"'S not true." Did I just say <u>snot true?</u> "Cuz I don't, you know, think that. I mean, you're okay, whatever." This was going downhill fast. "I just mean, I don't go around saying . . ."

Asia cleared her throat.

"Danny." Her voice was firm. "Forget about it. I don't even listen to that stuff."

"Oh. Good." But her quickness to dismiss it was disappointing, somehow.

"I've got to make a phone call," Asia took out her silver pocket watch. "I just wanted to say I'm glad you didn't do it. And I like how you defended Jasper. 'Friends and freaks forever!'"

She was quoting Rat Girl!

"How'd you know...?" I started.

Asia blushed. "Someone said you liked her."

"I do." I smiled. Were we still talking about Rat Girl?

Asia's smile deepened. "See you." As she turned around, her hair twirled around like a paintbrush.

She waved and floated down the hall, mysterious as ever.

What was she thinking? I had no idea.

But I knew that smile would stay with me for a long, long time.

* CHAPTER SIXTEEN *

Outside Comix Nation, I took a deep breath.
I hadn't been back since The Disaster. It
felt like a lifetime ago.

What would Logan do when she saw me?

I had to take the chance. My hands shook
as I opened the door and heard the familiar
jangle of the bell. The smell of 10,000 old comic
books flooded my senses — a bouquet of rotting

paper, microwaved nachos, and old bubble gum. If only they could bottle that!

Logan was talking on the phone. "...extra salsa with that," she said from her stool behind the cash register. "No — medium hot." She didn't look up from her manga book. "Black beans, not refried."

I forced myself to walk toward her. From somewhere above me came a terrible sound. "AAAWRK!" What was that?

I looked around.

"AAAAWRK!"

I looked to the right and saw Krazy Karl's parrot staring at me. What was _it_ doing here? Oh, right — Logan was hosting Karl this week, until he went back to New York. He was on a stool, buried in a comic book.

The bird had seen me, but Karl and Logan hadn't. I turned around. No way was I up for one of Karl's speeches! Tiptoeing back to the door, I tried to slip out without jangling the bell.

"AAAAAWRK!"

The bird squawked again.

Logan looked up.

"Danny!" she yelled.

I turned around slowly, letting go of the door.

"Logan, I'm really sorry —" I stopped.

She just stared at me. Her arms were folded, and her face was grim. I stood there, frozen in terror as the seconds stretched out.

"Come here," she said finally.

With wobbly legs, I walked to the counter. She grabbed my head and rubbed her knuckles into my scalp.

"Ow!" I cried.

After a flesh-searing noogie, she pushed me away.

"I know you didn't do it." Logan lifted her chin. "Asia called from school and told me what Axl said. So I called the principal."

Asia . . . told Logan?

"You're not off the hook, though," Logan continued. "You should have told me about the theft immediately — especially since you brought him here. So you have some responsibility."

"Absolutely." I gulped. "Anything you say."

"For the next three months, you'll work here at the store," Logan said. "For free."

Relief surged through me.

That was it?

"Fifteen hours a week," Logan continued. "That's like an after-school job."

I wondered if I'd misunderstood. Working at Comix Nation was a _punishment_?

* OTHER INEFFECTIVE PUNISHMENTS *

Video game testing

Pool guarding

Ice cream tasting

"It's not just bagging comics, you know," Logan said. "It's sweeping, dusting, mopping, setting mousetraps. Anything I want. Even laundering dirty costumes —"

That didn't sound good.

"Basically, you'll be my personal slave. And you know what?" Logan's eyes narrowed. "I <u>hate</u> slackers."

"All right. What's going to happen to Axl?" I dared.

"Ask him yourself." Logan shrugged. "He's outside, clearing gravel."

Axl was <u>here</u>?

"The principal brought him after school," said Logan. "Go."

Reluctantly, I opened the door and followed the path around to the little stretch of  concrete behind the store. Axl was sucking on a matchstick as he shoveled gravel into a wheelbarrow.

"Uh, hi," I said.

Axl grunted and wiped his brow.

"Is that your punishment?" I tried.

Axl spat out the matchstick. "Logan and the principal made a deal. I've got to clear all the gravel. Dump the trash. Clean up the alley. Paint the store. Put up a fence. It'll take months." Despite his chore list, he didn't sound nearly as angry as I'd expected.

"She made me a slave too," I said.

"And that's not all." Axl's voice changed. He sounded almost . . . proud. "She wants me to make the store burglarproof. From guys like me."

"Really?"

"Yeah. I mean, who knows more about break-ins? I can really help her out."

"Good," I said.

Axl took out another match. "Did you think you were getting your butt kicked?"

I nodded.

"Boris and Spike wanted me to ice you. For putting us on loudspeaker, and all. But Logan made me promise to leave you alone." He rolled his eyes.

"Oh, uh ... thanks."

"Don't get excited." Axl filled up another shovel. "While I'm here, I go by her rules. But when I'm done..." He flashed an evil grin.

I smiled back. "Nice to know nothing's changed."

"I'll see you later," Axl said importantly. "I've got to make those racks shoplifter-proof." He walked away, pushing a wheelbarrow and humming a violent rap song.

I couldn't believe I was walking away without so much as an arm burn. Maybe my real punishment was having Axl around to annoy me with threats — even if he couldn't act on them yet.

I wish they made greeting cards for occasions like this.

When I got back inside, no one was around but Krazy Karl. He was behind the counter, stroking Jennie the parrot. I tried not to make eye contact.

"Logan left you a work schedule," he said. "On the counter."

"Thanks." I picked up the paper and shoved it into my sketchbook. As I fumbled, the sketchbook fell to the floor. Being around Karl made me nervous. I remembered him lecturing me, and everyone laughing.

The book had fallen open to one of my drawings.

"What's that?" Karl pointed.

"Nothing." I scooped it up. "My sketchbook."

"Hand it over," he barked.

Reluctantly, I gave it to him. Karl put his glasses on and leafed through my sketches.

"AAAAAWRK!" squawked the bird.

Karl didn't say a word. I stood there

awkwardly, not knowing where to look. Finally, he cleared his throat.

"Excellent garbage barge," he announced. "My favorite part is the fish skeleton."

Hey. That was actually . . . a compliment!

In the pantheon of Stuff I'd Always Remember, getting props from Krazy Karl was way up there.

Karl paged through my whole sketchbook, stopping to remark, "Good chicken bone," or "I like the way you draw vomit." Wow — this was more like it! He noticed all my little touches — bloodshot marks on an eyeball, the stitching on a zombie's cheek.

It was amazing.

"You remind me of me when I was your age," Karl said, his voice gruff. "I was an art geek too."

"People called you a geek?" I asked.

"People?" he grumbled. "'Geek' was _my_ word. To me, it was the highest compliment."

Interesting.

Suddenly, I couldn't wait to get back to

school the next day. There was something I needed to do.

"What underwear are you rocking?" Giggle, giggle.

"Danny and Asia! Danny and Asia!"

As I walked down the hall, people yelled things and snickered. Annoying, but I didn't care.

I was looking for someone.

During passing period, I waited in the main hall, watching for noisy groups of girls. Finally, I recognized a towering coil of black hair.

"Chantal!" I called out.

She was telling a story. "So I said, 'Boy, what part of "You got bony chicken legs" don't you understand?'" A trio of girls whooped beside her. I tugged her sleeve.

"What do you want?" She spun around, annoyed.

I was out of breath. "A favor."

She motioned for the girls to go ahead.

"Danny Shine." She frowned. "What crazy tale you got today?"

"Will you put me back on the Loser List?" I burst out. "With 'geek' next to my name, like before?"

"What???" Her eyebrows drew together.

I remembered Karl saying "geek" was the highest compliment. Look at the trouble I'd gotten into getting my name off the list.

Why deny who I was?

"I'm proud to be a geek," I said. "Geeks are interested in stuff. They have weird ideas and creative minds, and if they don't always dress well it's because they've got bigger things to think about, like designing spaceports, having a Beatles tribute band, or winning the Frisbee Golf

World Cup. They wear calculator watches and bad sweaters. Get over it."

"Hmmm." Chantal frowned. "If people want to be on the list, what's the point? Besides, that list is gone. Shakima painted over it with purple nail polish. So you'll have to find some other way to let people know what a crazy oddball nutcase you are."

"Okay." I shrugged.

I couldn't wait.

H.N. KOWITT has written more than forty books for younger readers, including Dracula's Decomposition Book, This Book is a Joke, and The Sweetheart Deal. She lives in New York City, where she enjoys cycling, flea markets, and gardening on her fire escape.